I

CASEY BLAKE
ADVENTURES

# THE Crystal COBWEBS

SHARILEE ROE

THE CRYSTAL COBWEBS
Copyright © 2024 by Sharilee Roe

ISBN: 978-1-4866-2419-5
eBook ISBN: 978-1-4866-2420-1

Word Alive Press
119 De Baets Street Winnipeg, MB R2J 3R9
www.wordalivepress.ca

WORD ALIVE
—P R E S S—

Cataloguing in Publication information can be obtained from Library and Archives Canada.

To my Lord and Saviour Jesus Christ.
Without you, this book wouldn't exist. Thank you for not giving up on me!

In loving memory of Mona Moffat.
I miss you. Sorry this is late.

To my family and friends,
thank you for your love, support, and encouragement.

# Chapter One

Casey Blake groaned as she swung her legs over the side of the unfamiliar bed, hesitating a little in anticipation of touching the cold floor in her grandma's guest room. She could hear sounds in the kitchen below, and the smell of cooked bacon was starting to invade her senses. The rays of sunshine glistening off the drops of dew on the windowsill caught her eye. She glanced outside at the fog as it slithered back into the forest, leaving nothing but a shimmer on the ground. The mountains already seemed to be awake, stretching their peaks to the morning's golden rays.

The alarm clock next to the bed glowed brightly: 8:05 a.m.

*This can't be happening,* she thought. *It's summer vacation, a Saturday morning, and I'm up before 9:00 a.m. So much for sleeping in.*

Jumping up, she raced across the room to the cherrywood armoire. She grabbed for the drawer where she'd stored her warm, fuzzy socks the previous night. All she wanted to think about at this time of morning was warmth—and breakfast. Her stomach rumbled.

Casey shook her head, feeling slightly disgruntled. Right now she should be sleeping in and getting ready for some fun in the sun.

This summer it had been her turn to pick out where her family was going to spend their vacation. She got to set the agenda every third year. Last year, it had been her mom's turn, and she had chosen for them to go to Nova Scotia to visit her side of the family. The year before, her dad's choice had been South Africa.

She had chosen Florida so she could finally go see all the theme parks she was interested in. Her mom and dad had agreed to go when she was older, so that she could remember the experience. The time had finally come, as she had turned thirteen this year.

As usual, Casey had laid out a full agenda for the trip... only to have all those plans changed. Her parents, Jeff and Lexxie, had just been given a new assignment. They both worked for *The Chiselled Post*, her dad as a freelance photographer and her mom as a roving journalist.

Casey thought back to that fateful day when her plans for the summer had fallen apart. They had all been in the living room, her mom and dad sitting on the couch and looking over all the brochures Casey had collected. Suddenly the phone had started ringing and her mom had reached for the cordless receiver on the glass end table.

"Hello, Lexxie speaking..." There had been a pause. "Geneva? Yes, George, I understand. I'll just have to discuss this with Jeff and Casey first. Let me get back to you."

Casey had watched as her mom had gone into the kitchen with the phone. She'd sat up straight, straining to hear what was going on. George was her parents' boss. Casey could feel her dismay rising even before the truth was confirmed: Florida would be put on hold.

"No, Natasha went home for the summer already," her mom was saying. "Yes, Jeff's mom lives in British Columbia... I'm sure. I'll call you back ASAP... Okay, George, bye."

Natasha was Lexxie's twenty-five-year-old sister who had been visiting them in Edmonton, Alberta to conduct some historic research. She'd been a full member of the family for most of the past year. Casey loved having her aunt stay with them. She was like the sister Casey had never had, and Jeff and Lexxie thoroughly enjoyed her company too since they had so much space in their four-bedroom home. Plus, whenever Casey's parents went out of town on assignment, Natasha would look after her while they were gone.

Not this time, though. Aunt Natasha had left the previous week to go home to Nova Scotia for the summer. Which is why it had been decided that Casey would spend the summer in British Columbia with her grandma.

Casey pulled on her jeans and a T-shirt, then looked at her pale complexion in the mirror. She ran a brush through her wavy brown hair that fell just below her shoulders. Pulling it into a ponytail, Casey reflected on finding herself in Crystal Creek, B.C. for the very first time. Her grandma had bought this acreage only last year. The beautiful Victorian-style home was located right beside a lake. Well, that was pretty convenient! She just might be able to get some swimming in today before the public beach got too busy.

Eventually many of those beachgoers would come over to the old log cabin next to Grandma's house. The little building had been converted into a convenience store for the vacationers. She sold dry and canned goods, milk, pop, and ice cream novelties. The municipal campground down the road opened in June, which meant the store got pretty busy.

Finally, Casey went down the stairs into the kitchen where her grandma was standing at the stove making breakfast.

"So what do you think about worms and maggots?" her grandma asked.

"I hope you're not implying that those are my choices for breakfast, Gran!"

Her grandma turned and smiled at her. "Of course not, Cassandra. I was talking about the newest item I'm thinking of stocking at the store. You know, for the people who come in looking for fishbait."

Clara Blake had turned sixty-nine in March, although Casey didn't think she looked any older than her mid-fifties. She was always trying to keep up with the latest trends, which explained why she was sporting an emerald green T-shirt and blue jeans this morning. Curly brown hair, cut short at the nape of the neck, framed her slim face and her blue eyes sparkled, her dimples seeming to stretch the smile on her face.

She placed a plate of bacon, eggs, and hashbrowns on the table for Casey.

"Eggs overhard, bacon, and hashbrowns crispy," her grandma said. "There's toast in the toaster. It'll just be a minute. Did you have a good sleep?"

Casey grinned. "The bed was so comfy that I didn't want to move. And the smell of bacon did me in this morning. I guess it's actually after 9:00 a.m. now back home in Alberta, so I shouldn't grumble about it being soooo early." She looked around on the table. "Ketchup is in the fridge, Gran?"

"Yes, it's in the fridge door. You have a choice of red or green. I always find that you get the most interesting shades when you mix them together."

Casey raised one of her eyebrows, then shook her head as she got up from the table and crossed the room to the fridge.

"Honestly, Gran, sometimes I worry about you!"

Gran faked a shocked look. "You? Worried about me? You're way too young to be acting like your father! Oh, toast's up."

They both settled down at the table.

"Did you want to say grace, Cassandra?"

"Sure," said Casey. "Dear heavenly Father, thank you so much for today… and thank you for the food you have given us. Thanks for Gran cooking it. Please be with Mom and Dad on their trip, and keep them safe. In Jesus' name, amen."

"Amen. So what are your plans for today?"

"Other than stuffing myself with a great homemade breakfast?" Casey smiled as she put ketchup on her hashbrowns. "I'm not sure. Did you need me to help in the store today?"

"Oh no, honey. No. The store is in perfectly good hands. This is your vacation. You should enjoy it and have fun."

Casey raised her hands in resignation. Where did Gran get all her energy from? "Okay, okay, I'll stop offering to help. But do you at least want me to help you with the breakfast dishes?"

"Well… I suppose you could give me a hand. It would give us a chance to talk before I have to go open the store." Gran paused. "So tell me, are you planning on swimming today?"

Casey changed into her navy blue one-piece swimsuit and went searching for suntan lotion, which she found in the side pocket of her suitcase. Crossing the room to her black backpack, she also took out the latest book she was reading and retrieved her sunglasses from the vanity table. She glanced in the mirror, straightened her ponytail, and proceeded down the hall to the linen closet in search of a beach towel. Selecting a dark blue beach towel to match her swimsuit, she headed for the stairs.

As she was rounding the last step on the wooden staircase, Casey gave a start as the telephone on the stand next to the base of the stairs rang. She composed herself and reached for the phone.

"Clara Blake's residence. Casey speaking."

"Casey, honey, how are you?"

"Mom! Hi!" Casey dropped her things on the floor next to the stairs. "I'm fine. How are you and Dad?"

"Oh, we're okay. We both miss you a lot!"

"I miss you guys too. How was the flight?"

"It was really good. We didn't have too many layovers. We got into Geneva at 7:00 a.m., B.C. time, but your dad thought that would be too early to phone you, it being a Saturday and all."

Casey smiled. "Yeah, a little too early for me. Gran let me sleep in 'til 8:00. Her bacon dragged me out of bed, though. I was just going to head over to see her at the store before planting myself on the beach. Mom, you should see the place Gran bought!"

"So is it nice over there?"

"It's beautiful. She has an old Victorian-style house with a wraparound veranda that goes all the way around the side… there are two floors, plus an attic and a basement! My room has a door that opens up onto the veranda roof and I can walk around on it. It's so cool!"

"Really. It sounds pretty nice!"

"And the lake is beautiful," she said. "Gran loves her little store."

"Uh, hold on a sec. Dad wants to say hi."

There was a brief delay as she heard the phone being passed around.

"Hey, little squirt, how's it goin'?" her dad asked.

"Hi Dad! Everything is great. I miss you and mom, though. How are you?"

"We're both fine, but we miss you too."

Casey could hear a lot of noise in the background, as though her parents were in a crowded conference hall.

"I'm sorry, honey, but your mom and I just got paged. We're going to have to go. We'll call you tomorrow if that's okay."

"Sure, Dad."

"Look after yourself, and Casey…"

"Yes, Dad?"

"Please stay out of trouble and keep an eye on your grandma too. You two are like peas in a pod!"

Casey laughed. "Okay, Dad, but I don't think there's any trouble for us to get into out here. There's nothing around except for a lake. Oh, and a small town, but it's about eight kilometres away…"

"That's close enough. Just be good, okay? We'll talk to you tomorrow… and Mom's sending kisses. I guess we've gotta run. We love you, Casey."

"I love you guys too. Bye, Dad."

"Bye, Casey."

Casey sighed as she hung up the phone. She knew that God was watching over her parents, but she said a quick prayer for them anyway.

She took a moment to pick up her discarded items and left the house, walking over to Gran's store by following a well-worn path. The sun was rising in the clear blue sky, promising hot temperatures. It was already twenty-five degrees Celsius and it was only a quarter after ten. At least there was a slight breeze blowing in off the lake.

The door chimes jingled as she entered the store. On her right, she found Gran sitting behind the long cedar countertop. It had a glass display case so enormous that it anchored itself to the wooden floor. To Casey's left, she noticed a small rack for magazines and books. There was also a three-door cooler for the milk, pop, eggs, and meat. Canned and dry goods could be found down four different aisles, and a glass-top freezer at the back of the store contained frozen novelties.

Gran put down the book she had been reading. "Well, don't you look like someone who is all ready for the beach," she said, smiling. "Do you have enough suntan lotion with you?"

"Oh, I do. I brought a bottle with me from home. Thanks, Gran. I just thought I'd let you know that I'm going down to the beach. Mom and Dad called, by the way. They said hi."

"Ah, good. Glad they made it there safely. God is good, isn't He?"

"Always! So I guess I'll be outside, if you need me."

"Now you just quit fussing, Cassandra. Go and enjoy the sunshine. I'll find you later. Maybe we'll see about going into town this afternoon. How does that sound?"

"Sounds great!"

Casey couldn't help but feel a little excited. She hadn't had a chance to explore yet. All she'd seen of Crystal Creek was an aerial view from the plane as she'd flown towards the municipal airport just outside of town.

She found a spot on the white sandy beach and laid out the beach towel with precision, making sure that none of the corners were bent underneath. Kicking off her sandals, she wiggled her toes in the already warm sand and pondered how much smoother this felt compared to coarse brown sand.

She reached for her suntan lotion and put some on, making sure to get all the spots that would get lots of sun. If she didn't, she knew she'd be as red as a cooked lobster within half an hour.

Once the lotion was in place, she grabbed her book and started to read. She couldn't put it down. The female detective in the story had just found an important clue and she kept turning pages, rotating onto her stomach at some point.

> There she was following the suspect down a dark, cobblestone alleyway. The rain had finally stopped, but there was still no moon to light the way. She just had to get closer so she wouldn't lose him. The risk was high, but it would be worse if

the man figured out that he was being followed to his hideout.

She took a deep breath and silently crossed the street, trying to stay out of the light shining from the windows and dispelling the shadows. She strained her eyes as she stole across the court-yard, nearing the opening in the dark where...

Suddenly, Casey felt the hair rise on the back of her neck. A cold draft accompanied the extinguishing of the sunlight as she realized someone was standing behind her. Discreetly, she grabbed a handful of sand, ready to throw it in the stranger's face, and turned to face whoever it was who had stolen her sun.

# Chapter Two

Casey tried to catch a glimpse of the person standing in front of her, but it was hard to make out their features with the sun blazing all around them. She would have to make a choice—either drop the sand and shade her eyes so she could get a better look or…

"I sure hope you're not planning on using that!"

From the guy's voice, she could tell he was probably around her age. He also sounded quite amused.

Embarrassed, she slowly let the sand trickle through her fingers.

"Mrs. B. asked—oh, I mean your grandma… you are Cassandra, aren't you?"

He fidgeted as Casey stared up at him, speechless. He must have talked to Gran, she thought, since no one else would have known her full name.

"Please, call me Casey," she replied, getting up off the towel and marking the spot in her book before she put it down. "And you would be?"

"Matthew Barnett, but everyone just calls me Matt."

She noticed his smiling brown eyes first, then his sandy blond hair that looked like it belonged to someone who had been spending a lot of time in the sun. He was about thirteen or fourteen and a little taller than average, with an athletic build. He wore a burgundy T-shirt with an embroidered crest on the front. He had on a pair of well-worn jeans and sneakers.

She tried not to be jealous of his nice tan as she reached out to shake his outstretched hand. He seemed nice.

"Nice to meet you, Matt. You were talking to Gran?"

"Yeah, I was just in the store. She asked if I could locate a red granddaughter of hers on the beach, and ask if you're ready for a lunch break before you burn to a crisp."

Casey looked at her arms and found that they were turning a not-so-delightful shade of pink. She groaned inwardly. Why couldn't she tan normally?

"Out of curiosity, you wouldn't happen to know the time, do you?" she asked while trying to shake the excess sand from the beach towel.

"It's almost one-thirty."

"I've been out here that long? I'm surprised I haven't burned yet." She grabbed her book and suntan lotion.

"You do look like you've caught a little sunburn," replied Matt. "Maybe your grandma has something to put on that."

She started walking back towards the house. To her surprise, he followed along.

"So are you down here for a while?" he asked.

Casey stopped and turned to look at him again. "Just for the summer, as far as I know. Do you live around here?"

"You bet! I live over there."

She followed the direction of Matt's finger and landed on a set of buildings situated farther down the beach. There was a long dock with only a few boats tied up to it, as well as some paddle-boats and a seaplane. At the end of the dock was a little shop that looked like either a sports mercantile or a rental office. Probably both. And further inland a bit, an elaborate log house sat sheltered by some spruce and pine trees. It had a back yard enclosed by a fence, although the property looked like it extended far into the woods. Her gaze went up to the majestic mountain behind it.

"Wow, that looks really pretty," she said. "Is that your place?"

"It's home. If you want to rent a paddleboat or a canoe, you can come see me at the store by the dock. It's called Essentially Barnetts. We rent it all. My Uncle Pete owns the Grumman Goose over there."

"Excuse me? The what?"

"The Grumman Goose. It's a type of plane. It can take off from the water or it can take off from land, whatever's needed. It's pretty cool. You can fit about eight people in it. Uncle Pete flies contracts out to logging camps, resorts… anywhere someone needs to go. We also rent quads, motorbikes, and we also have trail rides. So if you like horses, I can introduce you to Maple, Storm, Duster… well there's a few there, anyway."

Matt shrugged his shoulders and started to kick a few of the stones around him with the tip of a shoe.

*So he's a little shy,* thought Casey. *Cute.*

"I guess we should go and see your grandma before she thinks I was absentminded and forgot all about you."

When they finally rounded the corner to the front of the house, Casey opened the screen door to the veranda. She could hear through the open window that Gran was already in the kitchen, retrieving articles from the fridge and placing them on the table.

Holding the main door open for Matt, Casey then entered the kitchen and placed her towel, book, and sunscreen on the bench by the door.

"Hi, Gran." She crossed the kitchen to help her grandma.

Gran looked up as she closed the fridge. "Well now, I see you have finally met someone from here." She smiled first at her granddaughter, and then at Matt. "So young man, I see that you have succeeded in locating my lost Cassandra."

"Gran…" Casey felt herself start to blush, even though her face was already red enough from the sun that no one would have been able to notice.

Matt sat on one of the stools by the counter. "You bet I did, Mrs. B. I think the reason she was lost, though, had something to do with the book she was reading."

"A good book is it, Cassandra?"

"So far, Gran." Casey went to the cupboard to get some plates to make sandwiches.

"Would you like to stay and have a sandwich with us, Matthew?" Gran asked. "Cassandra, can you get us a plate for Matthew, please?"

"In that case, I guess I'll be staying."

Matt exchanged his stool for a chair at the table. Casey had already retrieved an extra plate from the cupboard, having known her grandma would extend the invitation.

After they were all seated, Gran said grace, thanking God for friends, family, food, and a great day.

"So how is your family doing, Matthew? I see that your uncle came back from the Spruce Pass Logging Camp early this morning. Does he have to fly in and deliver more supplies?" Gran passed Matt a ham and cheese sandwich. "Don't forget to grab some of the veggies also. They're good to keep you growing."

"Thanks, Mrs. B. It all looks great."

Casey took the sandwich offered to her as well. "Thanks, Gran."

"Yes," continued Matt after he finished swallowing a bite of his sandwich. "Uncle Pete came in at about 5:30 this morning. He's waiting for some shipment that's due in town Monday afternoon and then he's flying back out with the equipment and extra supplies they ordered. He has to be back by Wednesday for sure because he has customers coming in from Ontario and they're headed up to bush country. I guess they have a log cabin up there by Lookout Falls."

"Lookout Falls… that *is* in the bush country. One must always make sure they're prepared when going up there." Gran paused thoughtfully. "And the rest of the business has been keeping you busy, Matthew?"

"Things have been pretty steady with the boats. A lot of visitors are going fishing lately, but Mom actually has a party of six people going horseback riding this afternoon at 3:00."

Casey reached across and took a couple of carrots to munch on while listening to the conversation.

When they were done, Gran took the empty plates to the sink and returned to the table with the jug of milk from the fridge.

"Who would like to go to town this afternoon?" Gran asked.

"I'd love to," exclaimed Casey, always ready for an adventure.

"Could I come too, Mrs. B.?"

"You can give your mom a call and see if it's okay with her. That is, if Cassandra doesn't mind."

"Oh, I don't mind, Gran. This way Matt can show me around Crystal Creek."

"Excellent. Then we can leave once you get the okay from your mom, Matthew. You can use the phone by the staircase there. That will give Cassandra a chance to change into some other clothes."

"Oh yeah, I forgot. I'll just be a minute." She bolted from the kitchen to the stairs, heading for her room.

"Cassandra…"

"Yes, Gran?" Casey halted on the staircase, leaning over the banister to hear her grandma in the kitchen.

"There's some skin cream in the main bathroom upstairs for that sunburn you've got. You may want to put some of it on before you go outside again."

"Thanks, Gran, I think I'd better. I sure hope it keeps me from peeling."

She took the rest of the stairs two at a time. After changing into a pair of shorts and a T-shirt, she put her bathing suit into the laundry hamper and placed her book on the corner of the vanity. Crossing the hallway to the bathroom, she fixed her ponytail and glanced through the cabinet for the cream. Once she spotted it, she proceeded to put some on. It was aloe with a mixture of flower extracts.

*Not too bad of a smell. I can handle this.*

She finished up quickly and put the bottle away.

Stopping by her room, she grabbed her purse and headed back downstairs. Matt had finished his phone call and was engaged in a conversation with her grandma. Upon seeing Casey, Gran picked up her truck keys and purse from the counter.

"Okay, we're all good to go. Matthew's older brother, Dylan, said he'd manage the store by himself until Matthew returns."

Gran locked the front door to the house and they walked over to the vintage 1943 Dodge pickup in the drive. She took a second glance at her store, seemingly to make sure she had hung up the closed sign in the window.

"Everyone, jump in."

Casey loved this old truck. It was a symbol of Gran, it seemed, and the very first vehicle Gran had ever owned. Her grandma had fixed it up over the years, getting it painted midnight blue, with white pinstriping, and changing the rims to nice updated chrome ones.

She jumped in and slid over next to Gran to make room for Matt to sit on the outside edge.

After all the doors were closed, Gran turned the ignition and the engine rumbled to life. Grins were exchanged as the truck slowly stopped at the end of the lane, then accelerated with renewed life as she stepped on the gas and turned left on the main road towards town.

The view along the road to Crystal Creek couldn't be described any better than to call it picturesque. There were so many different kinds of trees lining the roadside that Casey lost count as the truck wove down the hillside. Cows and horses were out grazing the lush green fields, oblivious to the aerodynamics displayed by the birds and butterflies. Fragrant smells floated through the truck as they passed a fruit orchard.

Before Casey knew it, the canopy of leaves opened up to reveal the tranquillity of Crystal Creek. It was a quaint town that seemed to have just one of everything. There was a large historic building at the south entrance of town, its monumental sign identifying its occupants as the town hall, police headquarters, and law courts. Across from it was the Crystal Creek Library. Down the road from the library, the elementary, junior, and senior high schools resided in a one-block radius. There was one food store, one pharmacy, one florist shop, one senior's lodge, and of course one Catholic church and one Protestant. Even every house seemed to have been built with enough of a difference between them to make each one unique.

Gran drove to the centre of town where the three main roads intersected. There in front of them was an old diner situated on the hill. The Malt Junction, as the lighted sign hanging on the post out front informed them. There was an island for vehicles to park around and Casey actually saw a girl, possibly around seventeen years old, come out of the building wearing a uniform and roller-skates to serve a customer.

"Am I really seeing that, Gran?" asked Casey.

"What's that, Cassandra?" Gran slowly drove the truck through the intersection, heading north towards Sam's Food Store.

"That girl in a uniform and rollerskates. It looks like something that belongs to the fifties."

"Oh, isn't that your sister over there, Matthew?" asked Gran as she glanced in the direction of Casey's gaze.

"Yeah, Amanda's working at The Malt Junction this summer. She really likes it there. She thinks it's cool to get paid to rollerskate."

"Cassandra, I'll have to introduce you to, Mabel, the owner. She would love to hear you say that you think the diner looks like it belongs in the fifties. She's been trying to keep it as authentic as she can. You'll have to see the inside of it. How about if we stop by there tomorrow after church for a bite to eat?"

"I think that it would be pretty cool," replied Casey.

"Good, it's set then. Tomorrow we shall dine in the diner!" Just then, they pulled into a parking spot in front of the grocery store. Gran turned the truck off. "Well, here we are. I'll be about half an hour. If you two would like to take a look around town, meet me back here?"

"Could we, Gran?"

Gran locked up the truck once they'd all gotten out. "Sure, dear. I've shopped here lots of times and won't get lost."

"Gran!" Casey bantered back. "Okay, I get the hint. We'll be back in half an hour." She turned to her new friend. "So Matt, where to first?"

"Well, let me see now. You've already seen most of the town, and you're going to The Malt Junction tomorrow, so… oh, I know where to go. Come on."

He turned and led her away from the store parking lot.

Casey followed her guide, trying to absorb everything as she went. Trees lined the sidewalk, giving them some shade from the afternoon heat. Lost in thought, she walked beside Matt, looking at all the old houses along the street as he gave her a tour of the neighbourhood.

Without warning, she stopped dead in her tracks. Taken unawares, she stumbled backwards and focused on the stranger suddenly standing in front of her. Despite the warm temperature, she felt a cold shiver course through her veins.

"Oh excuse me, I didn't see you," she said.

"Really now," the stranger replied. "What was your first clue, Einstein?"

Matt got between them. "Hey, give her a break, Darrin. She was just looking around and didn't notice you coming. I was giving Casey a tour of Crystal Creek. Casey, meet Darrin Masters."

"And what kind of a name is Casey?" sneered Darrin.

"It's short for Cassandra." She tried to smile at the glaring teen. "Everyone just calls me Casey. Well, except for Gran, that is... but you can call me Casey."

"A tour of Crystal Creek... so you're a visitor, huh? Maybe you should just go back to where you came from!"

"Actually, I can't, but thanks for the advice," Casey answered good-naturedly. She started to turn away from him, but then hesitated and turned back. "Oh, and nice to meet you, Darrin. Maybe I'll see you again sometime."

As she started to walk away, she began to smile to herself.

*Very interesting,* she thought. Had that been a flicker of surprise she had read in his eyes? He was actually a really cute guy. A little taller than her, with raven black hair and ice blue eyes. And icy they were.

Putting her thoughts aside, Casey fell in step beside Matt as they carried on down the block.

"Sorry about that," Matt apologized.

"Sorry about what? I was the one not paying attention to where I was going, Matt. So it was my fault when I actually bumped into him." She gave him a playful shove. "Plus, maybe God set things up to be this way."

"What, for you to bump into the neighbourhood grouch? Well, okay!"

"Hey, you never know. So anyway, Matthew Barnett, just where are you taking me?"

That question caused him to smile. "Just you wait. You've got to see this place." He grabbed her hand and broke into a jog. "Come on, Casey."

The excitement was becoming contagious. Casey started to laugh, and instead of being dragged down the road she decided it would be best to keep up with him.

Somewhere in the back of her mind, though, a pair of stormy, ice-blue eyes stared at her.

*So what is your story, Darrin? Just who are you, and what has made you so bitter?* She was determined to find out.

# Chapter Three

When they reached their destination, Casey stood in front of the immense amusement establishment in amazement. She couldn't believe what was right in front of her eyes. Who could have ever expected such a little town like Crystal Creek to have anything like this?

Matt was grinning like the proverbial cat who ate the canary. "Okay, you can close your mouth now."

"Oh, wow! This place has just about everything."

"Well, yeah, just about. Let me introduce you to The Light House! Outside they have go-carts, batting cages, and miniature golf. Inside there's ten-pin bowling and an arcade. Last but not least... drum roll please..."

"Brrrruummmpum."

"Thank you very much, ladies and gentlemen. Before us we also have the largest, and of course the only, waterslide in Crystal Creek."

"This is awesome. I can't believe it. Someone pinch me please." She winced. "Ouch! I was kidding, Matt. Actually, thanks, at least now I know I'm not dreaming."

"No problem, Casey."

"Man, this place looks cool. I'll have to ask Gran if I can come into town with you sometime and check it out. Too bad we don't have time right now."

But Casey soaked in the sights for a few moments longer. She just couldn't believe her eyes. Facing her was a long one-story building with a racetrack to one side and a miniature golf course on the other. Behind the building loomed the large waterslide and, from the splashing sounds she heard, there had to be a pool at the end of it. A short white picket fence enclosed the amusement park and instead of stone pillars marking the entranceway there was a five-foot-high lighthouse on either side.

"It's pretty great for our one-stop adventure shop," Matt agreed. "And if you really like fair rides, we have a fair that comes around every year for Canada Day. They stay for a whole week. What can I say? Overall Crystal Creek is a pretty cool place."

They turned and started walking back to Sam's Food Store.

"So what's the story with Darrin?" Casey asked nonchalantly.

"Angry, bitter, troubled... pick a word." Matt shrugged his shoulders and sighed. "I'm not sure what to say... he has issues? He just turned fourteen and seems to feel like the whole world is against him? Actually, I don't know what's eating him." He paused, thinking for a moment. "He was a pretty cool guy a couple of years ago, but then his grandpa passed away. Ever since then he's been pretty miserable. Nobody can even get close enough to find out what's going on. We've all pretty much given up. I mean, hey, who wants to have their heads ripped off for trying to be nice to someone who really doesn't seem to want to have anyone around?"

"Really? No way. How can anyone live without friends?"

"Honestly, Casey, watch out. He can be pretty vicious when he wants to be. I know that you most probably have a stubborn streak in you and won't listen to a word I'm saying, but trust me on this one. I mean it. Even I can't figure him out, and I've known him most of my life. Back when he was younger—well, before his grandfather died—we used to always hang out together."

"And how was he back then?"

"We had lots of fun. We had a club, built a fort, went to church on Sundays. He used to come out to my house a lot and we'd go treasure hunting."

"Let me guess… he's given up on God too?"

"Sorry to say so, but yeah, I think he has. He hasn't come to church in ages."

Casey shook her head sadly. "That's never a good thing, but we can look on the bright side. No matter where we are or where we go, God doesn't give up on us. He always has a plan. I wouldn't be surprised if He already has one for Darrin." She turned and made eye contact. "Speaking of plans, did you say something about treasure hunting?"

"Oh, yeah. Darrin used to tell stories of a lost town and buried gold. I think his grandpa told him those stories… and Darrin believed they were true." Matt's voice got quieter. "But no one has ever found a trace of this lost town."

"Matthew Barnett, are you pulling my leg?"

Matt smiled at her. "Cross my heart and hope to die… no, I'm not pulling your leg, Miss Cassandra—"

"Cassandra Blake, at your service," she said, grinning back at him.

*So there's an angry young man with a tale to tell,* she thought. *I wonder what that's all about.*

When they returned to the parking lot, she saw that her grandma had just walked out of the store with a cart full of groceries.

"Come on, Matt, race you back to the truck."

In no time at all, they were headed back to the house, each of them taking turns telling their exploits. Upon reaching their destination, Matt said goodbye and jogged back to Essentially Barnetts to allow Dylan a break.

Casey helped Gran unload the groceries and separate the ones for the house from the ones designated for sale.

With the set of house groceries put away, Casey and Gran carried the remaining items over to the store. As Gran unlocked the door and carried a bag of frozen items over to the freezer, Casey started unloading the rest. Her mind was so deep in thought, though, that she literally jumped when Gran spoke.

"Okay, out with it!"

"What?" Casey asked, confused. "I mean, out with what?"

"Out with whatever's been on your mind ever since we got home."

"Oh, it's nothing really, Gran."

"Come on, Cassandra. You know you can talk to me, don't you?"

Casey put another can of soup on the shelf. "Sure."

"Then please tell me, dear, before we have to rearrange the whole store."

Casey stopped and looked at the shelves in front of her, puzzled. She let out a small groan. "I'm so sorry! I'll fix it!" She looked down the aisle and inwardly groaned some more. "I'll fix all of it."

She couldn't believe what she had been doing. She had just been putting soup cans in the cereal section. And as she glanced down the aisle, she realized that she'd done the opposite there—cereal in the soup section.

"It's all right, I'll give you a hand." Gran began taking the misplaced soup cans off the shelf. "So do you want to talk about it?"

"What would it take for someone to lose their faith in God?" Casey asked after a pause. "I've been thinking about it and can't understand how someone could do that."

"Whoa, that is a pretty deep question. No wonder you've been distracted." Gran was silent for a moment. "Well, I guess they somehow felt that God had abandoned them when they really needed Him. Or maybe they felt that in some way God didn't answer their prayer, so it was like He had lied to them. But you know that God never leaves us or forsakes us. Romans 8:39 says, 'Neither height nor depth, nor anything else in all creation, will be able to separate us from the love of God that is in Christ Jesus our Lord.' Also, 1 Corinthians 13:7 says that love 'always protects, always trusts, always hopes, always perseveres.' God loves us and will always look after us. We just have to trust Him. So, out of curiosity, what made you think of this?"

"I guess you could say that I kind of bumped into someone today." Casey started to smirk in remembrance of that afternoon's meeting.

"And who, may I ask, was the recipient of this so-called meeting?" Gran teased.

"Just a guy. His name was Darrin. Darrin Masters, I believe."

"Ah. Now I understand. Hmm, now let me see, a tall lanky boy with jet-black hair and the bluest of eyes. Of course, how could I forget such a distinguished young man! So you ran into him today, did you?"

"Yeah."

"And how did that go?"

"I'm not too sure. He wasn't very friendly. He actually told me to go back to where I belong."

"Oh dear. I'm so sorry, Cassandra. I'm sure he didn't really mean it."

"It's okay. You know it takes more than that to stop me from trying to make a new friend. But Matt told me that Darrin stopped going to church after his grandpa died."

"That is true," replied Gran as she replaced the last cereal box onto the shelf. "Do you think the death of his grandfather has something to do with why he was so aloof?"

"Yeah. I'm not too sure what the real story is, but I'm thinking of trying to find out."

"Well, you just be careful. I know your heart is good, but please be a little bit cautious so you don't go and get yourself hurt. With some people, if they don't want your help, they can be spiteful. Besides, if it does have something to do with his grandfather's death, it may be a pretty touchy subject."

"I know, Gran. It's just that I feel that God wants me to reach out to him."

"All things are possible with God." She picked up the empty grocery bags and folded them as she walked over to the counter. "Thanks for all of your help, Cassandra."

"No problem."

"I'm going to be here until at least 6:00 p.m. Was there anything you wanted to do for the rest of the afternoon before supper?"

"Actually, I was thinking of going for a walk."

"Be back by 6:30 when supper's ready. That should give you some time for exploring."

"Sounds good to me. Thanks, Gran."

As the store bells danced behind her, Casey put her sunglasses back on to get a better look at her surroundings. She couldn't quite decide which direction to start walking. She could go see Matt at work... although he might be busy, judging from all of the activity around the dock.

Glancing back to the woods and the mountain, she finally made her choice. The wilderness would be an interesting place to start since it was the view that her bedroom window overlooked.

As she reached the edge of the meadow beside the house, she noticed a faint overgrown trail disappearing into the forest to her left. Curiosity got the best of her as she stepped forward onto the camouflaged trail covered in fallen leaves and pine needles.

She rounded a bend and kept walking, absorbing the peacefulness and suddenly feeling quite content. Rays of sunshine dodged the thick arms of the trees, spotlighting the trail in front of her. Squirrels scolded her and ran about trying to either distract her from their food stashes or play their own game of follow the leader.

Continuing down the path, she marvelled at the beauty God had created. Everywhere she looked brought on a fresh reminder of Him, from the birds flying overhead to the rabbits bounding from their lairs in search of food and the beetles scurrying about on the forest floor. She could also hear the sound of water flowing somewhere; she wasn't too sure yet where it was coming from, since the sound echoed through the woods.

A cool breeze whispered by, gently lifting the wisps of her hair. She shivered as the forest seemed to become denser, withholding the warm rays of the sun. The foliage was more abundant here and moss crept along the sides of the trail.

Just ahead, she noticed that the trees were thinning out. There must be a clearing ahead.

She picked up her pace, hastening to discover where the trail led—but all at once, the path vanished and was replaced with impenetrable brush and trees. Undaunted, she pushed the branches aside and burst through the undergrowth with such speed that she almost landed on her nose.

Casey straightened her dishevelled appearance and picked out what she could find of the twigs in her hair. With the task completed, she looked up to figure out what she had stumbled into—literally.

Goosebumps rose all over her body and she inhaled slowly, awestruck.

*Matt isn't going to believe this,* she thought as she rubbed her eyes and even pinched herself.

Nestled in the valley before her was a dilapidated town that had been lost in time. Some of the buildings were still intact, but others had fallen in on themselves. From the look of things, there had been a landslide on the east side, causing mass devastation. At one time, she figured it must have been quite the bustling place.

And it *was* real, despite her inability to believe what she was seeing. After all, it had passed the pinch test!

Casey picked her way down the gradual slope until she got to a wooden sidewalk bordering the main street. The boards creaked underneath as she walked along.

Peaking through the doorway of the first building, she deduced that it must have been the barber shop at one time. The high-backed chairs and mirrors were still there, with a porcelain sink in the corner. Everything was extremely dusty albeit still intact.

Looking to the far side of the street, she saw a row of buildings damaged by the landslide. She decided not to venture over there—not by herself anyway. She guessed that about ninety-percent of those structures had been destroyed.

Casey resumed her stroll until the boardwalk ended. She continued walking, crossing the road, and cautiously mounted the next boardwalk. She stepped onto it, testing to see if it would collapse under her weight, and found it to be in passable condition.

She tried to look through the windows of the next building and found them to be just a little too dirty. So dirty, in fact, that she suddenly had to sneeze.

After regaining some control, she caught a glimpse of a pair of doors a little farther down. She walked closer, wondering if they would be unlocked. She slowly placed her hand on the doorknob and turned. With a little bit of effort, the door mechanism gave way and it creaked open.

The sun shone into the room, bringing the cobwebs into focus; the way the light danced made them look like intricately woven crystal lace.

She gently moved the cobwebs aside and entered. Directly in front of her was an enormous wooden staircase. Just off to the left was a tall counter with a key rack positioned behind it. If she had to guess, this had once been a hotel—although the dust was so thick that obviously no one had visited in a long time. Every step she took left a record in the dust.

Skirting the velvet curtains that draped over the entranceway to the left of the front desk, Casey ducked into a parlour. The walls had wood panelling and floor-to-ceiling bookcases framed the fireplace. There were a few large chairs, which after inspecting Casey determined must have been upholstered with leather.

As she looked around, she started to imagine what it would have been like back in the day. She pictured the crackling of the fire as people strolled from the entrance to the upstairs rooms. In her imagination, others came down and sat in the parlour, dressed in their finest. Music played and guests chatted completely unaware of the passing of time...

Casey shook her head, rousing herself from her daydream.

She walked back towards the entrance, then kept going and crossed into another room. Brushing away some more cobwebs in the doorway, she entered a space lined with windows. Sunlight was trying to break through the filthy panes of glass, dimly revealing lavish wooden tables and chairs. What really caught her attention was the old player piano against the wall.

*Unbelievable,* she thought. *I wonder if it still works...*

She blew the layers of dust from the piano bench but quickly found herself out of breath. She resorted to trying to brush it off, then sat down with the job only partially accomplished, anxious to try playing the instrument. She pumped the pedals, and to her surprise music suddenly spread through the room, filling every corner. It was a soft, beautiful, haunting melody that made her feel like she was intruding on a stranger's memory.

With tenderness, she did her best to clean off the front of the piano, revealing the intricate craftsmanship of its woodwork. She squinted making out images of hummingbirds, flowers, and vines chiselled into the panel. She could hardly believe it!

As she reached across the piano to swing herself off the piano bench, the time on her watch caught her eye.

She jumped up, her mind starting to race. Where had all the time gone? It was already 6:18 and Gran had told her that supper would be ready at 6:30. She was going to be worried if Casey didn't get back in time.

She quickly exited the hotel, making sure to close the front door carefully behind her. If she slammed it shut too hard, she knew she'd have to find another way in later.

Stepping off the boardwalk, she opted for the dirt road dotted with sparse patches of grass. When she got to the edge of the abandoned town, she retraced her steps back through the underbrush, only stopping once to glance back and take a mental picture of the sight as she had first glimpsed it. The sleeping valley lay undisturbed.

Casey turned and ran down the forest path.

# Chapter Four

C asey pulled the screen door open and stumbled into Gran's house, late and breathless.

"I was worried that I might have to send the cavalry out to find you, dear." Gran turned around to smile as she retrieved the pizza from the oven. She had barely placed it on the counter when she rushed forward. "Cassandra, are you all right? Just look at your clothes. Did you fall? Did you hurt yourself?"

"I'm okay, Gran."

Pulling some more twigs and leaves from her hair, Casey kicked her running shoes off onto the porch and closed the door. "I'm just going to run upstairs and clean up for supper." She walked over to her grandma and gave her a kiss on the cheek. "Honestly, Gran, don't worry. Everything is okay. You won't believe what I found, though!"

"Don't forget to wash your hands while you're up there. I guess I'll just have to wait until you get back to find out just what you've been up to. Don't be too long. From the grin on your face, this info must be pretty good. I'm dying to hear what kept you."

Casey raced upstairs, sliding on the waxed wood floor in her room as she tried to come to an abrupt halt. She changed as quickly as she could then ran back towards the stairs only to realize she'd forgotten to wash up. With her stomach growling in anticipation of the pizza, she dashed to the bathroom. Once she felt satisfied with her appearance, she returned to the kitchen to find her grandma already seated at the table. Casey crossed the kitchen and joined her.

"So, are you going to tell me?" asked Gran as she finished saying grace.

"You're not going to believe it, Gran. Even I find it hard to believe."

"Okay, Cassandra, you've got me. The suspense is killing me!"

"I found an old ghost town."

"You've what?" Gran dropped her pizza. Luckily her plate was still underneath it.

"When I went for my walk this afternoon, I found a trail over by the forest out front. So I decided to follow it, and the next thing I knew it ended at some bushes. I pushed through and found this town in a little valley. It was as if it was just sleeping there. It was about a forty-five minute walk from here, and from the looks of it the town was hit from a landslide."

Casey took another piece of pizza.

"Did you say a landslide?"

"Yeah… I mean yes, Gran."

"Seems to me someone once told me about Crystal Creek not being the same as it used to be. Do you think maybe that's what they were talking about? I mean, that would make sense if the place you found was the original Crystal Creek. Maybe they had to move and rebuild it."

"That would make sense considering the things Darrin's grandfather was telling him about a lost town. Do you think that explains it?"

"I'm not too sure, dear, but I think it's quite possible. The only way to know for sure is to find something there that could tell you the name of the place. And maybe Darrin could tell you some of the stories his grandpa used to tell…" She trailed off, deep in thought. "Cassandra, dear…"

"Yes, Gran?"

"Please take Matt or someone else with you next time. In case something happens."

Casey smiled at her. "For you, Gran, anything!"

Rising early the next morning, Casey joined her grandma for breakfast. The sun was shining and she was excited about the day ahead. They discussed going to church and then stopping by The Malt Junction afterward for a bite to eat. Other than that, they didn't have plans.

While getting ready for church, Casey climbed out of the shower and wrapped a towel around her wet hair. She secured a second towel around her body, then opened the bathroom door and crossed the hallway to her room.

She sifted through her Sunday clothes and finally picked something to wear. It was her knee-high blue floral print dress with a V-shaped neckline. The thing she liked most about it was its light material, which made it perfect for this summer heat. She also liked the bell sleeves that hung loosely around her wrists. She put on the dress and pulled some of her curls back with a clip.

Finishing up, she picked up her Bible from the vanity and grabbed her sandals as she left the room.

She entered the kitchen and hopped from one foot to the next as she put on her sandals. Gran was sitting at the table, all ready to go.

"I like that peach dress on you, Gran."

"Why thank you, my dear. I must say that yours is quite charming also." Rising from her chair, Gran picked up her belongings from the counter. "Shall we?"

"You bet."

Later that morning, Casey sat quietly in church listening to Pastor John's message on Mark 4:21–25 and Luke 8:16–18. It was about whether people would place their light on a table for all to see or cover it up. Would they tell others about their faith in Jesus, or would they feel ashamed.

She thought about Darrin and how much she wanted to tell him that she cared—and God cared too.

As Gran and Casey left the church and headed for the truck after the service, Casey spotted Matt just ahead of them. She waved.

"Hey, Casey," he said. "How's it going?"

"Awesome, and you?"

"Things are cool. So you and Mrs. B are going to The Malt Junction for lunch?"

"You bet, young man," said Gran. "Did you want to join us? I believe Cassandra is bursting at the seams to talk to you."

Gran nudged her gently in the side.

"Gran!" she said, a little embarrassed.

"Sure thing, Mrs. B," Matt replied. "I'll just have to check with Mom and Dad first. I'll be right back."

With that, Matt took off in search of his parents. Casey watched as he found them by their vehicle. She saw an older boy with them and the waitress she had seen at The Malt Junction.

"That must be Amanda and Dylan over there, right, Gran?"

"Yes, I believe so."

Matt came running and Gran waved back to the Barnetts.

"I assume this means yes," Gran said.

"You bet, Mrs. B. I'm all yours!" He grinned. "Let's eat!"

They all laughed as they piled into Gran's pickup.

Matt opened the door for them at The Malt Junction. Scanning the room for an empty table, Casey spotted some booths near the back of the diner.

"I see that you found a good spot near the jukebox," Gran said, sliding onto the cushioned bench seat.

All around the diner were artifacts from the 50s and 60s, down to the checkered black-and-white tile floor. Pictures of movie stars and singers hung on the walls.

A woman wearing a mauve poodle skirt, black leather belt, and white short-sleeved dress shirt approached their table. She was probably in her sixties, but Casey felt that she looked younger with her honey-blond hair neatly arranged in a French roll and a flowing scarf tied around her neck. Even her footwear was vintage black-and-white saddle shoes.

The woman arrived at their table. "Why hello, Clara. Long time no see! How have you been?"

"Just peachy," said Gran. "And how about yourself, Mabel?"

"Busy as always, but isn't that the best way to be?" Mabel answered cheerfully. "And who do we have here with you today? I recognize young Matt, but what about the little lady next to him?"

"This is my granddaughter, Cassandra. Jeff's daughter."

The woman reached across the table to shake Casey's hand. "Hi, my name is Mabel."

"You can call me Casey. It's nice to meet you!"

"And you as well. Your grandma has told me so much about you, so it's nice to finally put a face to the stories. I understand you may be visiting for the whole summer?"

"Yes, as far as we know."

Gran winked at Casey. "And I'm sure that Cassandra will find more than enough to keep her busy while she's here in Crystal Creek."

At that precise moment, Matt's stomach let out a loud growl. They all started to laugh—that is, except for an embarrassed Matt.

"Well, on that note I should bring you guys some menus before you starve to death," Mabel teased just before walking away.

Matt sat there looking very sheepish, a crimson blush creeping up his neck and flushing his cheeks.

"Don't tell me that was Matthew Barnett's stomach I heard," a voice said.

Casey looked up just in time to notice a young girl around her age appear behind Gran. Apparently the sound of Matt's stomach growl had carried as far as the booth next to them.

"Oh," Matt said. "Hi Petra."

Her almond-shaped brown eyes sparkled. "A little hungry, are we?"

"Casey, this is Petra Lee. Petra, this is Casey Blake," said Matt, making the introductions. "And you know Mrs. B."

"Hello, Petra dear," replied Gran. "You played the flute wonderfully this morning in church. That is quite a talent you have."

"Thanks, Mrs. Blake."

"Petra and I go to school together and were in the same class last year," Matt explained.

"And rumour has it that we're in the same class again this year," Petra said. "Mrs. Jones will be our homeroom teacher."

Matt groaned. "I heard she's really brutal."

"She's not that bad, Matt," Petra chided. "Are you taking music this year?"

"Yeah, I'm going to try the guitar again. You?"

"I think I'm going to learn the violin."

Gran smiled. "That would sound pretty in church."

Matt turned to Casey. "Petra is a music prodigy. She can play just about any instrument you give her. She's her own band."

"Well, I don't know how to play the violin yet," Petra remarked.

"Yet," Matt interjected.

At that moment, Mabel came back to take their order. Casey chose the chicken fingers with fries and a side salad. Matt, of course, picked his favourite, the Malt Junction Supreme—a char-broiled burger with mozza cheese and mushrooms, with fries on the side. Gran ordered the Caesar salad topped with grilled chicken and fresh Parmesan.

As soon as the food arrived, Gran said grace.

Gran squeezed her lemon into the glass of ice water. "So, Cassandra, would you mind it too much if I went over to the Lodge this afternoon to visit some of my friends?"

"Sure, Gran," Casey said as she coated her fries with ketchup.

"I'd expect that you and Matt already have plans."

"You bet."

Petra poked her head above the vinyl-upholstered bench again. "Boy, you live life dangerously, Casey Blake."

Casey just about choked on her fry. "Hey, Petra, do you want to come with us this afternoon?"

"Where are you guys going?"

"Yeah! Just where *are* we going?" Matt asked.

"To the old ghost town," Casey whispered with a twinkle in her eye, feeling the excitement envelop her.

"The what?" he cried out loudly.

"Shhhh."

"Yeah. Shhhh, Matt!" Petra turned to her. "Did I hear you correctly?"

"I said… a ghost town," Casey whispered. "And Matt, you can close your mouth now."

"When? Where? How far? Is it real?" The more questions Matt asked, the squeakier his voice became. Petra, Casey, and Gran burst out laughing.

"Sure, I'm in." Petra paused and looked down on her side of the bench. "It's okay with you and mom?" she asked her parents.

Casey heard some inaudible voices talking, then Petra nodded and confirmed that the plan was a go.

Matt nodded so rapidly that Casey automatically thought of a woodpecker going after a bug in a tree. Casey split into laughter again.

"You'd best slow down there, young Matthew, before you lose your head," Gran warned, apparently having the same thought.

"It's a little too late for that," ribbed Petra.

Matt made a face at her.

"When you've all finished eating, I can take you back out to the house," Gran said. "You'll want to change out of your church clothes before you go exploring."

Matt muffled out a "You bet, Mrs. B" as he tried to finish his lunch in a hurry. Gran smiled as she elegantly rose from their booth to pay the bill and chat with Mabel.

Wiping off his mouth with a napkin, Matt looked over at Casey. "So you really found it? The lost town that Darrin's grandfather talked about?"

"Well, I'm not too sure if it's the one he talked about, but I am sure that it's a town that looks like it has been lost to time."

The three of them got up and walked towards Gran, who was now waiting by the front doors. As they quietly discussed what they would need to take with them on their adventure, Casey felt the tiny hairs on the back of her neck start to stand up.

Even when they reached the doors, the feeling hadn't gone away.

She became nervous as she tried to remember just how loudly they had been talking. Had someone overheard them discussing the ghost town?

Before leaving, Casey stopped to scan the restaurant for the cause of her sixth sense going berserk. Her eyes finally locked on an elderly woman who happened to have been sitting in a corner booth near to where they'd been seated. As the woman realized she'd been spotted, though, she quickly looked down to write something on the newspaper spread out on her table.

Trying to shake her unsettled feelings, Casey went outside and began crossing the parking lot.

Suddenly, she slammed into someone.

Casey groaned as she staggered backwards, realizing that she hadn't been looking where she was going.

"Well, if it isn't Einstein again!" said Darrin, his blue eyes sparkling mischievously.

# Chapter Five

Embarrassed, Casey tried to compose herself. She reached down to smooth her dress as it ruffled in the breeze. "Hello, Darrin."

"My, don't we look nice today." His steady gaze was examining her from head to toe.

Casey glanced over his shoulder to Matt, who was rapidly waving his arms. She choked back a laugh; now he looked like a windmill!

Darrin followed her gaze and suddenly his back stiffened. "I guess you should be getting back to your church buddies," he spat out. "I won't detain you any longer."

With that, he stormed past her towards the restaurant.

"Darrin, wait! It's not what you think." She reached out and grazed his arm.

He stopped, staring down at her hand.

She removed it, almost as though he were a snake about to strike.

"Matt's just excited," she explained. "I found a ghost town yesterday, and we're going to explore it this afternoon. Would you like to come with us?"

Casey could see Matt's crestfallen look when he realized what she was doing, but she knew in her heart that it was the right thing.

Darrin had a look of total shock on his face, although the shock quickly transformed into hatred.

"You told her, didn't you, Matt!" he called across the parking lot. "So it's just a big joke between all of you stupid Bible thumpers?"

"No, wait," Casey said. "It's true, Darrin. I found it yesterday in the valley by Gran's."

Darrin kept backing up, his expression full of disbelief and anger.

"Hello, Darrin Masters," came a calm, soothing voice.

*Gran,* Casey thought. If anyone could make him listen, it would be her.

Darrin fidgeted as he looked down at the cement. When he looked up, he had an apologetic expression on his face.

"Hello, Mrs. Blake." This time he sounded sheepish but respectful.

"Now, I know that you don't want to believe my granddaughter here, but I do."

"Have you seen it then?"

"Not at this moment. Not yet."

"Then how exactly do you know that it really exists and that she's not lying to you?"

"Because we have taught her that it's not right to lie. Not even a white lie. It is the ninth commandment God gave us. You can read it in Exodus 20."

"Well, I *don't* believe her," Darrin insisted. "God left my family and me alone a long time ago. He doesn't care about us, so I don't care about what He has to say!"

And with that, he disappeared into The Malt Junction.

Casey could feel the air slowly defrost as her body absorbed the sun's rays. Gran walked closer, put her arms around Casey's shoulder, and led her to the pickup truck.

"Maybe you're right about him blaming God for the way some things have happened," Gran remarked. "God is probably working on thawing his heart right now. Just be there for him. God will do the rest."

Gran smiled encouragingly and squeezed her shoulder.

Upon reaching the truck, they all piled in.

"So, Miss Petra Lee," said Gran, "To your house first?"

"Wow, yes! I forgot all about changing out of these clothes."

Petra was in and out of her house in five minutes, then jogged back to the pickup. When she jumped back in, she was breathless with excitement.

As Gran drove back home, Casey looked out the window, her thoughts returning to her confrontation with Darrin.

*If anyone can reach him, it's You,* she prayed silently. *Heavenly Father, you know why Darrin is hurting. Please break down the walls that are guarding his heart. Please let him get to know You better and entrust his life to You. Thank You for caring about us and for letting me meet him. If there's anything I can do, please let me know. In Jesus' name I pray, amen.*

They soon arrived and Matt sprinted off towards his house. Casey and Petra paused to watch Gran drive away again, off to visit her friends at the Lodge.

Casey immediately ran up to her bedroom.

"Do we need to take some flashlights with us?" Petra called up the stairs.

Casey was already half-changed and hopping towards the armoire to find a T-shirt. She struggled to pull on a pair of jeans.

Would they need a flashlight? It was quite bright now, so it probably wouldn't come up. But just in case they ended up somewhere where the sun didn't shine…

"Sure," she said as she hurried down the stairs, now dressed in scruffier clothes. "We'd better take a couple, just in case."

Casey pulled her hair back into a ponytail with a hair elastic as she walked to the kitchen pantry and glanced around for flashlights.

She located two of them on the bottom shelf. She smiled as she realized her Gran had a Swiss Army Knife there as well. She put it in her pocket, wistfully thinking about her parents in Switzerland. Even though she knew they were doing well, she sure missed them.

"What are you thinking about?" Petra asked.

She looked up. "Oh, I'm just thinking about my mom and dad. They're on a job in Geneva, Switzerland… so I'm staying at Gran's until they get back."

"Wow, Geneva! I'd like to be able to go there."

"Maybe you will one day, considering your talent for music. I can picture you playing Europe's great concert halls."

"Really? You think so?"

"Of course!"

The screen door suddenly opened, causing both Petra and Casey to jump as their eyes darted over to discover who the culprit was.

"What are you guys doing?" Matt asked. "Just standing around? We've got things to do, places to go, things to see!"

Petra and Casey burst out laughing. They picked up the flashlights and went outside.

"What took you so long?" Casey asked, grinning at Matt.

He feigned shock. "What? I had to run all the way to my house, then change and run back. You're the ones who were just chatting away…"

Petra placed her hands over her heart, miming as though she'd just been hit there. She mock-staggered around on the lawn.

"Oh no, Casey, he got us. Aaargh. I don't know if I'll be able to live with the thought… knowing…"

"Okay, you two," Casey said. "Come on. We don't have all day."

She started running towards the path that led into the bush. It was barely visible unless you knew exactly what you were looking for.

Carefully picking her way along the path, Casey continued around the bend, dodging rocks and overgrown foliage. When she realized that she was suddenly alone, she stopped and turned around.

Matt's voice echoed through the trees. "C'mon, Petra. I wouldn't want to get left behind out here."

"Who said anything about getting left behind?" Petra asked as she stumbled into Casey.

As Matt stood there laughing, Petra ran her fingers through her long, straight, liquorice-black hair and brushed her bangs out of her eyes.

"Well now," he said. "I thought I had seen my share of slackers, but you two take the cake. First you stand around in the kitchen talking, and now you're just lying around. We'll never accomplish anything with this type of work ethic."

Matt turned away with a big grin on his face and started to stroll down the trail.

"Ohhh! Let me at him," exclaimed Petra.

She staggered to her feet while trying to brush herself off. Casey only held Petra back for a second before deciding to join her in chasing Matt down the forest path.

Upon reaching the end of the trail, Matt looked at Casey inquisitively. "Okay, so where is it?" he asked. "This is just a dead end."

"To you it's a dead end, Matthew Barnett, but to me it's just the beginning." She leaned forward to pull back the obstructing branches on one of the trees that guarded the path.

Suddenly they detected a flash of movement in front of them. Startled, Petra screamed.

"I think we just scared that ruffed grouse," Matt said, laughing. "Maybe we should call it the *ruffled* grouse instead."

Petra groaned. "Oh, that was a bad one, Matt."

"I'll agree with you there. Well, come on you two." Casey pulled the branches away again and they walked through the underbrush into the clearing.

"Wow, Casey!" Matt exclaimed. "This has to be it!"

Petra could only agree. "Wow is right!"

Casey started down the rocky hillside towards the town as Petra and Matt followed. Retracing her footsteps, she tried to take the same path as the day before. Once again she got onto the boardwalk and strolled past the barbershop and the post office.

"Hey, check this out!"

Casey turned at the sound of Petra's voice, which seemed to be coming from inside the barbershop. Matt and Casey soon joined her where she stood holding an old newspaper.

Petra turned the newspaper around so they could read the headlines. They both moved closer to peer down at the yellowed, fragile paper in her hands.

THE CRYSTAL CREEK GAZETTE
*where we press the facts*

They all gasped when they saw the date: January 13, 1927. Scanning the articles on the front page, Casey suddenly spotted something interesting near the bottom of the page.

> Last night at 7:23, quite the commotion erupted at the Crystal Creek Hotel, and Doc. O'Reilly was summoned. He emerged from the entranceway at exactly 8:10 to happily announce the birth of Edmond and Amelia's first child. They have named their son Brandon Daniel Masters, who weighs a healthy 7 pounds and 2 ounces. When we spoke to Edmond Masters about the birth of his son, he

was quite ecstatic that he now has an heir with whom to share the family fortune.

In reference to the family fortune, the Masters' Crystal Creek Hotel is quite a gold mine by itself. With the latest gold vein discovered last month, the hotel has been booked solid by newcomers to the area.

The article continued on to detail how much gold had been found recently, including the fact that some miners had been staying in the hotel until their own houses could be built.

"This is it, Matt," Casey remarked. "It has to be the proof we were looking for. This must be the same lost town that Darrin talked about."

Matt nodded in agreement. "So do you guys want to check out the hotel?"

By the eager grins on all their faces, Casey bolted through the doorway and ran down the boardwalk, keeping the newspaper with her so she could show it to Darrin and Gran later on.

Crossing the road, she quickly found herself in position to open the hotel door. Carefully she turned the rusty doorknob as it emitted a low, squeaky groan. The door opened to reveal the cobwebs that guarded the entranceway.

"Is this ever cool!" Matt said as they entered.

Casey smiled. "I know, Matt. Can you believe that this has been here the whole time?"

"Hey, Matt, check out this room!"

Casey turned to see that Petra had stepped into the parlour. Her voice floated out from behind the burgundy velvet curtains.

As they joined her, Matt seemed to be marvelling at everything in sight—the petite Victorian chairs, the fireplace, the bookcases…

Petra sat in one the chairs and pulled a book from the nearest shelf. She began flipping through its pages.

"I could really get used to a place like this," she murmured.

"Ditto," agreed Casey. "Hey, do you want to see something really cool?"

"Sure!" chorused Petra and Matt.

They immediately followed Casey out of the room as she crossed over to the doorway that led into the dining room.

As soon as she saw it, Petra ran over to the player piano and began scrutinizing it to see if it would still work.

"I think it still works," Casey said. "Just have to pump the foot pedals."

Upon finding the pedals, Petra proceeded to activate the piano's mechanisms. The more she pushed the pedals up and down, the more the tracker bar turned. The silence in the dining room was suspended in time as the mystical melody slowly filled the air.

Listening intently to the song, Casey found herself almost hypnotized as she watched the music roll turn and the piano keys dance up and down as though by magic.

Matt was the one to break her trance. "Hey, that's kind of a nice tune, isn't it?"

"Yeah," Casey said as the music faded away. "I wonder what it's called."

"It was very pretty," Petra stated as she turned on the piano bench to look at Casey and Matt.

Matt glanced around the rest of the dining room. "Hey, can we go check out some more of this place or what?"

In agreement, the three of them headed to the back of the room where a hanging curtain concealed a corridor that led into the rear side of the building. They turned on their flashlights and proceeded along the hallway, with various doors branching off to the left. Opening one showed a passage back to the lobby and the elegantly carved staircase near the front desk. Another door opened into what seemed to have been a linen closet.

A little farther along, the hallway ended with a narrow staircase on the right—probably the one reserved for the staff's use. There was also a doorway to the kitchen and the pantry, and another door along the back wall, next to the pantry, that led outside. On the other side of the kitchen, a different hallway returned them to the front of the hotel. Investigating this one, they found a small room on the right with a table and a few chairs.

"I bet you the servants all got to eat in here, eh?" guessed Matt.

Casey nodded. "Most probably. It's pretty close to the kitchen…"

"Hey, don't they get a bathroom?" Matt sounded indignant.

"Yeah, there was a small one back there with a washbasin and a towel rack," Casey told him.

Petra shrugged. "It must have been the size of a closet, because I missed it."

Before Casey could respond, Matt was running back to the front of the hotel and the main staircase. "Race you to the top floor!"

When the girls reached the third floor, they looked around and tried to spot Matt. Suddenly, his head poked out of a room at the end of the hall.

"Down here," he called.

Casey quickly entered the spacious bedroom. It had a mahogany four-poster bed, an armoire, two dressers, and a vanity table to match. She also noticed a red velvet settee in front of the large window, which had a beautiful view of the mountain. To the left of the window, a door led out onto a balcony. There was also a private bathroom with an old porcelain tub.

"This has to be the Masters' bedroom," Matt pointed out as he looked through the drawers of a wooden rolltop desk.

"Hey, what's this?"

Glancing over his shoulder, Casey scanned the items in front of him. "Looks like some personal stationery and letters. They seem to belong to Mr. Edmond Masters."

"Oh, look." Petra gently pulled out some sheets with music notes dancing across them. She fingered through them delicately, then stopped on one of the sheets. "Wow. This one is called *The Sweetheart's Melody*, by Edmond Masters, dedicated to his sweetheart Amelia. I think this is it… the song that was playing on the piano downstairs." She examined the page more closely. "Although something doesn't seem quite right…"

Casey joined Petra in taking a closer look at the music sheet. "What do you mean?"

Petra pointed at a line of musical notes. "Well, there's something odd about this bar. Do you mind if I take these back with us? I want to check it out later."

Matt and Casey both nodded in agreement.

Without warning, a door slammed shut somewhere down below. They all froze.

Casey could feel her heart pounding and her hands cramped up from her death grip on the flashlight. Petra looked terrified too, and by the fear on Matt's face, Casey realized it was up to her to figure out what to do. She turned and stealthily made her way to the hallway. If someone else was in the building with them, she had to find out who it was.

# Chapter Six

Casey quietly crept down the hallway till she was standing at the top of the stairs. Glancing over the oak bannister, she scanned the area below, searching for any movement.

"Do you see anything?" Matt whispered suddenly into her ear.

Casey jumped. "Don't do that. Warn me next time... you just about gave me a heart attack!"

Looking behind her, she found that Petra had also joined her.

"Sooo, did you see anything?" Matt asked again.

"No," she whispered back. "I'm going down there."

"I'm coming with you."

"So am I," Petra replied timidly.

Trying not to let the stairs creak, they all headed down to the main floor. When they got there, Casey looked around the lobby.

"I think it came from over this way," Casey said, pointing the direction with her flashlight. She started walking towards the kitchen pantry.

Petra seemed unsure. "Are you sure we should be doing this?"

"It's okay, Petra," came Matt's hushed voice. "We'll protect you."

"You? Okay, now I'm really scared." Petra joked, trying to regain her composure. "You'll watch out for me won't you Casey?"

Casey looked back with a grin. "Well, of course."

Matt was already heading down the corridor towards the kitchen. "Come on, you guys."

Peering over his shoulders, Petra and Casey looked at the closed door to the servants' dining room.

He cautiously turned the doorknob and opened the door slightly. He then took a deep breath and quickly opened it the rest of the way.

Casey's gaze darted around the room, checking it for any signs of an intruder. She noticed a long tapestry flapping in front of an open window. Nothing else in the room seemed to have been disturbed.

"A gust of wind must have blown through the half-open window," she said.

Matt nodded. "You're probably right."

"Well with the dimensions of the window and with the velocity of the wind…" Petra trailed off as she made eye contact with Matt. "Uh, yeah. Sorry, guys. You're most probably right, Casey, is what I meant to say."

Casey smiled. "At least now I know who to see about quantum physics."

Laughing away the paranoia, they headed back into the main hallway, where Matt's stomach let out an enormous growl.

"Whoa, is it that time already?" he said. "I thought we just had lunch."

Petra looked down at her watch. "Actually, Matthew Barnett, it's now 4:27.".

"4:27!" Casey looked down at her own watch in surprise. "I guess we should start heading back."

"I should be getting home," he replied with a grin on his face. "Plus, supper should be happening shortly."

Petra shook her head. "Good old Matt. You can always count on him to tell you when it's mealtime."

"Hey, can I help it if I'm a growing boy?"

Casey opened the front door to the hotel and came face to face with Darrin on the boardwalk outside. Matt and Petra piled into her from behind.

"Hey Casey, what did you stop for?" Then Matt saw who it was. "Oh. Hi Darrin."

"Matt," Darrin answered warily.

Darrin peered past them into the lobby. "So I guess you weren't lying, were you, Einstein."

"Nope!" Casey said. "But hey, since you're here, do you want to see inside your great-grandfather's hotel?"

Darrin looked at her blankly. "My great-grandfather's?"

"Well, if your grandfather's name was Brandon Daniel, then this is his father's hotel."

Darrin entered the hotel, brushing aside a few more of the cobwebs, much to Casey's enjoyment; she sure didn't like the thought of so many spiders running about. He walked over to the front desk.

"There's a parlour over here," Petra showed him, pulling back the heavy drapes.

"And on this side, there's a dining room," Matt said with a gesture. He started waving his arm like a salesperson. "Here we have many tables and chairs for the guests and patrons of this beautiful establishment!"

Petra started to laugh. "Come on, Matt, you're gonna make me feel like I'm on a game show."

"So Matt said your grandfather used to tell you stories?" Casey asked, turning to Darrin. "What were they about?"

"Well, about Crystal Creek. But not the Crystal Creek I knew. He used to talk about how his dad and mom used to live in the biggest house in town."

"He sure had that right," Matt commented, although he clammed up when Petra gave him a look to be silent.

"And he used to tell me how there was a great treasure his father had saved for us," Darrin added.

"A treasure?" Casey asked.

"Yeah, but I thought his stories were all lies. He talked about an old town, and I never saw anything like that before he died." Darrin's tone of voice changed from ponderous to bitterness. "Well, there *is* one thing he lied about. He always talked about there being a God!"

Casey frowned. "Why would you say that?"

"Because if there is a God, He would have heard the prayers I asked. He would have saved my grandpa instead of taking him away from me!"

"I'm sorry, Darrin. There's nothing I can do to take away this pain you feel, but you're wrong about there not being a God. There is a God, and the truth is that He really does care about you and He does hear our prayers, no matter who we are."

"Yeah? Well, I guess I'm just not ready yet to believe you, Einstein!" With that, Darrin stormed out of the hotel.

Casey paused while looking at the open door, remembering that she had forgotten the newspaper upstairs. "Hey, you guys go after him and I'll catch up to you. Try and talk to him, Matt. He's hurting and he might just want a friend."

"What are you going to do?" Petra asked.

"I'm just going to run upstairs and get that newspaper that I forgot on the rolltop desk."

"Okay. Don't be too long."

"Back in a flash."

Casey darted up the stairs. When she got to the room, she glanced out the window and saw that Matt and Petra had caught up with Darrin and they were all talking.

*Heavenly Father, I don't know what Your plan is, but please let us be able to reach out to him,* she prayed. *He has so much pain and has decided to put the blame on You. Please help us to befriend him so he can see Your love for him through us. In Jesus' name, amen.*

As she picked up the newspaper and headed back for the door, she suddenly got the distinct feeling that she was being watched. Her arms broke out in goosebumps and the hair on the back of her neck stood up.

Casey warily walked to the doorway of the bedroom and peered down the corridor, but she couldn't see anything out of place. The hallway was completely deserted except for the solitary antique grandfather clock that stood in solemn defiance near the top of the grand staircase. Giving herself a shake, she decided that she was probably just psyching herself out.

*With God on my side, what should I fear?*

She was about to start for the stairs, though, when her attention was drawn to the dust that lay by the servants' staircase. She gingerly walked across the patterned carpet and looked down. There were definitely footprints.

Casey swallowed. They had not been alone.

Taking a closer look, she hesitantly put her foot next to one of the prints. It looked to be around the same foot size as hers, maybe just slightly bigger. And it looked skinnier. Was it a woman's shoeprint?

Her thoughts ran back to The Malt Junction earlier that afternoon and the woman who had been looking at her. Was this her shoeprint? And if so, why would she have followed them here? Why not say hi or otherwise let them know she was there?

"Casey? Are you coming?" yelled Petra from down below.

"Yeah!"

She ran down to meet up with her friends, but she only got as far as the landing on the second floor when she heard a deafening bang echo through the hotel. She froze as Petra let out an ear-splitting scream.

Panicking, Casey stumbled down the final flight of stairs to find Petra at the bottom, white as a ghost.

"Are you okay?" Casey asked.

Petra was as wide-eyed as a spooked deer. She nodded slowly and pointed down the hallway. "I think it came from that staff dining room again," she whispered.

Casey led Petra behind the large oak staircase and down the hallway. She opened the door and peered inside for the third time that day. Scanning the room, she noticed that the wind had knocked a chair over. The long tapestry in front of the open window was now flapping with greater fervour as the gusts of wind picked up.

"It's just the wind again," Casey said as she walked over to the window. "I'm going to close it."

She reached up, trying to pull the old frame down into place. After a few tugs, the weathered wood moaned as it moved. Satisfied that it was closed, she turned to leave.

Petra let out a sigh of relief. "Sorry, Casey, I don't mean to be so jumpy. I sure thank God that you were here. I don't know what I'd do if I had been by myself."

"You would have hightailed it out of here."

She laughed. "You've got that right."

Suddenly the boys ran into the hallway, out of breath.

"Are you guys, okay?" Matt was quick to ask.

"Yeah, we heard a noise and then someone let out a blood-curdling scream," added Darrin.

Petra looked down sheepishly. "Sorry, guys, the scream was mine."

"And the noise you heard was most probably the door slamming again," Casey replied pointing behind them. "The wind seems to be picking up."

"It looks like we may be in for a rainsquall pretty quick here," warned Matt.

Darrin nodded. "We were just about to come in and let you know… but the scream was kind of distracting."

Petra sighed. "Sorry."

"That's okay, Petra, we understand," Matt teased. "You being a girl and all."

"Hey!" She turned to Casey and handed over the music sheets. "Could you hold onto these for a moment please?"

Suddenly Petra gave chase to Matt, who darted out of the hotel.

Casey and Darrin paused only long enough to carefully close the front door behind them. Casey placed the music sheets inside the newspaper as they started down the wooden boardwalk.

They quickly caught up with Petra and Matt, who were already at the edge of the valley. Climbing back up the hill towards the path, Casey glanced up at the sky behind them to see the approaching storm.

Darrin followed her gaze. "It's coming in pretty quick."

"Maybe if we hurry, we can get back to Gran's before the rain starts."

*Tap-tap-tap.*

The sound was so quiet at first that Casey barely noticed it. What was that?

"Run faster!" exclaimed Darrin.

Casey turned to him with an expression of shock. "What?"

"Come on," he cried, grabbing her hand as they started to run through the branches onto the forest trail.

Surprised and confused, Casey stumbled along, clenching the flashlight and papers to her chest. As she ran, watching for obstacles along the rough path, she realized that the sound of the tapping was getting louder and faster. The rain was starting to fall in big fat drops, tapping the leaves and falling to the forest floor.

When they broke through the forest and entered the meadow, they made a beeline towards Gran's house.

Bursting through the entranceway, they staggered onto the front porch just in time as the rain became a torrential downpour. Darrin found a lawn chair and sat down as Casey and Petra collapsed onto the porch swing. Matt doubled over, trying to catch his breath.

"Wow. That was sure fast, eh?" Matt straightened up and ran a hand through his wet sandy blond hair. Finding an empty lawn chair by the door, he sat down.

The door to the house opened and Gran looked outside. "I thought I heard some voices out here. Would anyone like a towel to dry off?"

"Yes, please," they all cried in unison, which brought a smile to all of their faces.

Gran disappeared inside but returned shortly with a handful of towels. As they were drying off, she went back into the house to make some hot chocolate.

Another gust of wind howled past the house, bringing with it more rain.

"I think we made it just in time," Petra said as she pulled the towel off her hair, the damp black strands all askew.

Casey smiled as she looked around at her newfound friends.

*This is quite the interesting group You have put together, Lord. Please be with us and bless this friendship. In Jesus' name, amen.*

Gran pushed the screen door open with her foot as she balanced a tray of steaming mugs with both hands. Darrin rushed over and held the door for her.

"Why thank you, Darrin, much obliged." Gran made her way over to a small table beside the porch swing and put down the tray.

Darrin flashed her a dazzling smile. "No problem, Mrs. Blake."

"That's my boy," she said, patting him on the shoulder before vanishing back into the house.

Petra acquired a cup and warmed her hands with the mug. "Mmmmm. Hot chocolate."

"So what do you think, Darrin?" Matt asked.

"I think the hot chocolate is a nice touch," he said.

Casey just about choked on the mouthful she had been about to swallow, not having expected that comment from Darrin. Coughing and sputtering, she tried to think of an answer. "I'll have to agree with Darrin. Mmmm. Rich hot chocolate."

Casey and Darrin exchanged glances and she caught the twinkling in his eyes.

"I meant about the ghost town," Matt said, trying again. "Do you think that all those stories your grandpa told you were true?"

A frown creased Darrin's forehead. "I don't know. I mean, I guess that they're true… but…"

"But what?" Petra spoke up in a soft voice.

"Well, it's just that… oh, never mind." Darrin placed his empty mug on the tray. "I should get back to town. It's almost suppertime already. Mom and Dad will be expecting me."

Petra jumped up too. "Oh, wow! My mom and dad will flip if I'm not back soon."

"Yeah, they'll send the cavalry out to find you," Matt teased her.

Darrin leaned close to Casey. "Her dad is a cop," he explained.

Before they all went their separate ways, Matt stopped them. "Hey, since we're on the subject of cavalries, could I ask you guys a favour?"

"What is it, Matt?" Casey asked.

Matt nervously scuffed his shoe on the wooden veranda floor. "Well, you can say no if you want to, but I was thinking…"

"Yes?" Petra prompted.

"All right. Thanks, Petra. I'll see you guys tomorrow morning! Bright and early now, okay?"

Matt started to walk down the steps from the veranda, leaving them totally puzzled.

"Matthew Barnett! You just hold it right there!" came a very commanding voice from the usually timid Petra. "Just what do you mean by that?"

Shrugging his shoulders, Matt looked at them pleadingly. "Well, it's just that Mom asked me to exercise some of the horses tomorrow so I just thought that if you all gave me a hand... please?"

"Oh, I hate it when a guy has to beg," Petra replied. "Oh all right, Matt. Count me in."

Casey was excited, but tried to stifle it. "I know what you mean, Petra. But I guess you can count on me too."

They all turned to look at Darrin, holding their breath.

Darrin looked back at each of them. Suddenly, a smirk pulled at the corner of his lips. "Well, I suppose I could try to make it out tomorrow morning. On two conditions."

"Name them," said Matt eagerly.

"Number one is that it can't be too early..."

"Is 9:30 okay for everyone?" Matt looked around, and they all nodded; it would be fine.

Darrin didn't flinch. "And number two is that I want to ride Bandit."

"Bandit it is!" Matt reached forward to shake Darrin's hand in agreement.

The deal was closed. They would go for a ride tomorrow morning and Casey was thrilled.

Matt said a quick good-bye and raced out into the rain.

A few minutes later, Gran emerged from the house. "Would you two like a ride home? It would be a lot faster and drier than walking back to town."

Petra and Darrin looked at each other. "Yes please!" they replied in stereo.

Suddenly remembering something, Petra ran over to the porch seat and retrieved the music sheets. "I almost forgot! Thanks for holding on to these, Casey."

"No problem," she said, following Petra and picking up the newspaper. "And I almost forgot something too. This paper is for you, Darrin. You might want to keep it."

Darrin looked down at the article on the front page. A smile came to his face. "Thanks, Casey, I think I will."

"Well, see you guys tomorrow morning then," Petra said as they walked to Gran's pickup which had already roared to life.

Casey nodded. "You bet! Bright and early."

"See you in the morning, Einstein," added Darrin.

And with that, they were gone.

Casey waved at the departing truck as it slowly made its way down the road. Gran turned left and the truck soon disappeared behind the row of weeping willows that guarded the valley road.

Pondering the latest events to herself, she went about collecting the dirty mugs and towels before taking them into the kitchen. She placed the cups into the sink, then walked down the hallway to deposit the towels in the laundry room.

A few minutes later, she crossed back to the kitchen and filled the sink with soapy water. All the while, she couldn't help but smile to herself about Darrin getting the chance to see the ghost town for himself.

*Heavenly Father, You do work in amazing ways.*

Another round of rain pelted the house, causing Casey to look out the open kitchen window. The view looked out over the veranda and Gran's store.

She frowned. *I sure hope it isn't this wet out in the morning or it sure is going to be a muddy ride.*

# Chapter Seven

The pesky mosquito buzzing beside her ear was starting to drive Casey crazy. Still half-asleep, she swatted the air around her head. The noise persisted. Annoyed, she sat up, rubbing her eyes, and looked around for the culprit.

"Oh no!" she exclaimed, kicking her sheets back and jumping out of bed to turn off her alarm clock. It hadn't been a mosquito at all; in fact, it had been her alarm.

She glanced at the clock and then peered outside to check the weather. Overcast. And the clock stated that it was already 8:32, which meant the alarm had already been going off for at least two minutes.

There was a soft tapping on the door to her room.

"Yes?" she called.

The knob slowly turned and Gran peeked around the heavy wooden door. "Good morning, Cassandra. I see that you're finally moving." She smiled at Casey. "I have some porridge made if you'd like some."

"Thanks, Gran. It sounds great."

Casey got up and moved across the room to the armoire.

"Oh, and it's a little cool out there this morning, so you'll want to take a sweatshirt with you for the ride. Also, if you guys are going up into the mountains, remember that it's usually chillier there."

Casey held up a powder blue T-shirt and soft lilac sweatshirt. "Do you think this will be okay?"

"If it starts to warm up, you can always tie the sweatshirt around your waist," Gran said, nodding. "I'll meet you downstairs."

When the door was closed again, Casey yanked a pair of blue jeans from out of an overstuffed drawer. She hurriedly got dressed and darted into the main bathroom to freshen up. She decided to leave her hair down this morning but lifted up the strands in front of her ears and fastened them with a clip. A few of the shorter tendrils fell loosely to frame her face.

Taking one last look in the mirror and feeling satisfied with what she saw, Casey grabbed her sweatshirt and ran downstairs where she found Gran in the kitchen, sitting at the table.

"The porridge is still hot and on the stove. Just help yourself."

"Thanks, Gran."

Casey went over to one of the cupboards and retrieved a bowl, then got some cutlery. After spooning up a bowl of porridge, she proceeded to plunk herself down on one of the wooden chairs beside her grandma.

Gran said grace, and then Casey dug into her steamy bowl of porridge. The milk was warm and the brown sugar on top was fully melted.

"I guess you're not too sure how long you'll be out riding for today," Gran said.

"No, I'm not. I assume it'll be for a couple of hours anyway."

Amusement lit Gran's face. "Actually, knowing that Matthew Barnett, I think I might expect you to be back around noon..."

Casey laughed as she poured herself a glass of orange juice. "I think you might have a point there. I think he has a built-in dinner bell."

"That is, unless his mom packs a lunch for you guys."

"Do you think she'd do that?"

Gran pondered this for a moment. "It's always a possibility with Mrs. Barnett. She's a pretty nice young lady who loves to go on trail rides and presenting her customers with a picnic." Getting up from the table, she crossed the wooden floor to pour herself another cup of coffee. "So whenever you return is fine with me. Just let me know that you're back. You'll most probably find me in the store."

"Okay. Well, I guess I should get going." Casey rose from her chair and placed her dirty bowl and glass into the sink. "Bye."

She kissed Gran on the side of the cheek, then pulled her sweatshirt on as she shoved her feet into her sneakers.

She walked outside of the house and inhaled a breath of fresh mountain air. Looking around, she started down the path towards the lake and noticed that the sky was still quite overcast. The puffy clouds were a mixture of greys, blues, and whites. Grimacing, she hoped the weather would clear up.

Casey felt a little chilled as she walked by the still water. The mallards were out, enjoying their swim in the quietness of the morning. Their movements were echoed in the reflection of the water as they went about their daily routine.

"Hey, wait up!"

She turned to see who had called to her and saw Petra quickly closing the distance between them on her mountain bike. Casey waved and then stopped as Petra rode up and climbed off the bike.

"So are you ready for the ride this morning?" Petra asked, her midnight black hair swishing in a ponytail that was secured at the crown of her head by a bright yellow elastic.

"I think so. I just hope that my clothing will be warm enough." She looked down at her lilac sweatshirt and jeans. "I've got a T-shirt on too, in case it warms up."

"Ah, yes! The power of positive thinking!" Petra unzipped her black hooded fleece jacket to reveal a fluorescent yellow crewneck. "I've come prepared also."

Casey shielded her eyes as they started to walk again. "Whoa, that's bright. Close the jacket... I can't see!"

Petra giggled as she zipped it back up. "Just think! If we get lost in the mountains, at least they'll be able to send a search party to find us."

"You could be our little beacon of hope," Casey said, smiling.

"Yup!"

All of a sudden, Petra's words sank in. "But what do you mean, *if we get lost?*"

"Huh? Oh, I was just kidding." Petra stopped walking and paused, "Well, actually—"

The sound of a very loud engine starting up interrupted her. Spooked, they both jumped and looked at one another in shock. They burst out laughing at each other's expressions. It was just the Grumman Goose, the plane parked out by the dock in front of Matt's family's store, preparing for take-off. The pilot was testing the wing flaps and revving the engines. Casey could just make out the pilot's face—a young man wearing a baseball cap and sticking his head out the cockpit window.

Movement on the dock caught her eyes, and when she squinted she noticed Matt standing under the wing. He seemed to be talking with the pilot. But as soon as the plane started moving away from the dock, Matt backed up.

"Looks like Pete is heading out today," said Petra.

Casey's attention was fixed on the plane as it turned on the water. It rapidly glided across its mirrored runway, creating a trail of waves as it gained momentum and soared upwards into the sky.

The plane was quite interesting as the bottom looked like the underside of a boat; it had no skis, though it was equipped with landing wheels that tucked into the side of the plane and could be deployed if the pilot needed to touch down on land.

As she watched, the Grumman Goose vanished into the low-lying fog between the mountain peaks. The ducks and geese in the plane's path quickly dispersed only to regroup once again in its wake. The hypnotic waves lapped against the shore, putting Casey in a kind of trance that was broken by the sound of Matt's footsteps clunking across the wooden dock.

"Hey! You guys made it!" Matt exclaimed cheerfully as he jumped onto the beach. His sneakers crunched the pebbles as he closed the distance between them.

"Morning, Matt," Casey called back.

"Is this early enough for ya, Barnett?" Petra asked, teasing.

He smiled as he came to a halt in front of them. "Had a hard time getting up this morning, Petra?"

He stood there with his thumbs hooked into his pockets. His worn jean jacket hung open, revealing a black T-shirt underneath.

"Actually, if you really want to know, I was up early this morning." Petra glanced first at Casey, then back at Matt, who had cocked his head a little to the side. It seemed as though he was waiting for a confession. Petra suddenly caved, shrugging her shoulders. "Okay, okay. I woke up early because I was so excited about the ride and I couldn't get back to sleep."

Matt patted Petra on the back. "Doesn't it feel so much better now that you've gotten that out?"

Petra jokingly tried to punch him in the shoulder, but he dodged.

"Hey Matt, did Darrin show up yet?" Casey asked as she looked around in anticipation of seeing Darrin's mischievous smile.

Disappointment briefly crossed over his features. "Actually, I haven't seen him yet. But he'll be here soon. I'm sure of it."

Casey said a silent prayer that Darrin would show up before they had to leave.

The shop, Essentially Barnetts, was built partially over the water, making it look a bit like a marina. It was anchored on pilings and overlooked two different docks jutting out into the water, each one extending out about twelve feet. In front of the shop was a wooden boardwalk that joined the docks together. There was also a second entrance to the store, at the back of the building, with stairs that led down to the beachfront.

At the moment, the shop was quiet. Customers were getting a late start on this hazy Monday morning. But soon there would be a lot of action.

Skirting past the wooden boat racks, laden with canoes, Casey, Matt, and Petra ventured on towards Matt's house.

"Do you guys want to head out to the stable to see the horses while we wait for Darrin?" asked Matt as they stepped onto a well-worn path that guided them inland.

"You bet!" Casey was so excited that she started to lead the way, but then stopped as she realized she didn't have the slightest clue on where she was going. Looking back over her shoulder, she spotted Petra and Matt trying to stifle their amusement. "Sorry, guys. After you, of course."

Matt gave Casey a grin as he sauntered past.

Walking in front of a few pine trees, Casey quickly found herself on a dirt road. The smell of burning wood drew her gaze towards the rock chimneys on the house in front of her.

"It's amazing!" Casey exclaimed, awestruck by the enormous house. It was positioned on a hill, set back from the road. The manicured green lawn sloped down towards a rock wall that separated it from the road.

As they walked alongside the wall, Casey noticed that an entranceway had been dug out of the incline; a rock stairway had been added in its place that led up to the house. Flowers lined the walkway, and other flowerbeds were located strategically around the lawn.

By the looks of it, she would have guessed that someone around here had a green thumb and a love for horticulture!

The two-storey log house reminded her of a rustic farmstead, with guest cottages dotting the hillside in the background. A wooden deck lined the front of the house, partially sheltered by the second-floor terrace. French doors opened onto that terrace, giving people access to a grouping of lounge chairs and tables. A wooden patio swing, chairs, and side tables were spread around the deck below. A large picture window beside the front door sported an "open" sign, and through the window she could see into a dining room.

The smell of bacon wafted over to them.

"Mom's cooking for the breakfast hour this morning. Then Dad's taking over for lunch in the restaurant so Mom can take some riders out this afternoon."

Carrying on down the road, they were quickly greeted by two friendly dogs. Matt explained to Casey that the shaggy Bernese Mountain dog was named Rocky, after rocky road ice cream—his mom's favourite flavour. The other dog was called Oreo; the black-and-white border collie was at that moment wagging his tail like crazy and panting his hello to Casey as she patted him.

The dogs took off ahead as they walked up the road and entered another valley. Before them lay a pasture enclosed by trees and the mountains behind it. A couple of brown jersey cows grazed after their morning milking amongst the horses.

A feeling of excitement once again overpowered her and she picked up her pace. Jumping a fence, Matt opened a gate to lead them through the pasture to the stables situated to the right of the fence line. The red and white building's large double doors were already open, giving some of the animals free rein to roam about.

"Yipes!" Petra exclaimed, just about tripping over a kitten that had darted out from its hiding spot. Suddenly four more kittens came from the same direction, in the midst of their own game of hide and seek.

"This here is Gypsy," Matt said, introducing them to a chestnut Arabian. The horse stuck her head out of the doorway and leaned against the half-door, nickering a hello.

"Wow is she ever pretty, Matt," said Petra. "It is a girl, isn't it?"

Chuckling, Matt nodded as he patted Gypsy's neck.

Petra reached forward and stroked the white stripe that ran the length of Gypsy's face, from the top of her forehead to just above her nostrils. The rest of the horse was a deep red chestnut colour except for the four white socks, the whites of which extended just below each knee to the hoof.

"Is it okay if I ride her?" Petra looked at Matt with such a pleading expression that Casey had to bite her lip to keep from laughing.

"Sure, Petra. She's a pretty good horse and I think you're experienced enough to handle her."

With that, Petra actually hugged Matt. He started to blush, then tried to hide it by backing up and turning away from them.

"Which one do you think you would like to ride, Casey?" he asked.

Casey looked about at the horses in their stalls. There were so many that she didn't know which one to choose. "Can I come back every day and ride a different one so this decision won't seem to be so difficult?"

"If you wish." Matt gave her a reassuring smile and turned to Petra. "You can too, if you like."

Petra's eyes lit up.

"And here's Bandit," Matt said, shyly changing the subject.

They looked into a stall to discover the tall Pinto that had started to move around to face them when he heard his name. The markings on the horse's face created patterns that looked like a mask over its eyes and under its jaw. In a way, it reminded Casey of the Lone Ranger. The horse also had a black patch covering his nostrils, mouth, and chin. Casey wondered if it was just her or if Bandit had found a pail of hair dye and dunked his mouth in it...

"I assume this is why you named him Bandit," she said.

Matt laughed. "You'd think that, but actually Mom gave him the name because when he was just a colt he always tried to steal the apples she picked and put in her basket. When he nabbed one, he'd just stand there eating it as if to say, 'Are there any more on that tree?' Mom thought it was so funny."

Curious about all the activity around him, Bandit poked his head out and sniffed each of his visitors, letting out a soft neigh. When Matt picked up the small bucket of oats that had been placed outside his stall, the horse nickered excitedly; knowing what came in that pail, he pressed himself up against the stall door. He even tried to nibble the bucket closer to him.

They all laughed at these antics, and Matt eventually gave in and moved the bucket closer.

The sound of a motorbike outside perked their attention, including Bandit's, who dug his head from out of the bucket. He quit munching and flicked up his ears.

A moment later, Darrin emerged from around the side of the stable with the dogs following him. He walked into the stable and joined the group.

"I knew you'd make it!" Matt said.

Casey silently prayed a quick *Thank you.*

Bandit snorted and pawed at the straw in his stall, anxious to be noticed as well. Laughing, Darrin stepped forward and gave the horse a few firm pats on his neck.

"Hey, old buddy," Darrin said. "Did you miss me?"

Bandit nodded his head as if he'd understood the question. They all laughed at that.

Darrin turned and noticed their smiles. "So what are we all waiting for? Let's go riding."

Matt patted Darrin on the shoulder as he glanced over at Petra and Casey. "Petra chose Gypsy to ride. That means you've got Bandit and I'm taking Napoleon. All we have to do is find a horse for Casey."

Casey looked around at the other stalls and spied a white horse. As she walked towards it, the horse inside came forward and stuck her head out over the stall's door. Her face was white with a tiny bit of grey on her nose. Upon further inspection, Casey found that it was dappled grey on its rump, had a dark grey mane and tail, and had four grey socks.

The horse smelled her outstretched hand and bobbed its head.

"That one is our Andalusian. She's named Storm, and by her reaction I'd say she's picked you," Matt said.

"I'm going to grab the brushes and picks," Darrin remarked.

He walked back down towards the other stable entrance and disappeared into a side room.

"All the tack, brushes, and stuff are located there if you need anything," Matt explained.

Darrin quickly returned with two containers. One he gave to Matt and Petra, because their horses were next to each other at the opposite end of the stable.

"We can share this one," Darrin said to Casey.

"Sure."

They quickly burst into a flurry of action, getting their horses brushed and the hooves cleaned for riding. Casey enjoyed the care she was taking, making sure there were no stones lodged under Storm's hooves. She didn't want to take the chance of her new-found friend going lame.

With short, even strokes, she brushed the dust and dirt out of Storm's coat. Then, when Matt showed up, he handed her Storm's saddle blanket, which she threw over the horse's back, centring it over her withers.

Matt handed Casey the bridle as he proceeded to put the saddle on the horse. "You know how to put the bridle on?" he asked.

"Yup, no problem."

Casey was careful with the bit, trying not to clunk Storm's teeth. She reached up, fixed it behind the ears, and pulled the strap down, doing up the buckle near the horse's jaw. She pulled the long grey mane out from under any restraints so it could flow loosely.

"Looks like you're ready to take her out," Matt remarked as he opened the door for them.

Leading the horse outside, Casey joined up with Darrin and Petra, who were already seated astride their horses. She stopped Storm for a moment to recheck the saddle and ensure it was cinched up enough. Finding it all right, Casey positioned the reins in her hand, placed her foot into the stirrup, and hoisted herself up.

Matt mounted Napoleon, who happened to be a very regal-looking pure black Friesian.

"So we're all set?" Matt asked.

They all answered in the affirmative, so Matt set his horse into a walk, aiming for the gate that would let them out of the pasture. Without even getting off Napoleon, Matt had the horse go through manoeuvres that enabled him to open the gate.

Once they had all passed through, Matt closed the gate and proceeded down the road. Casey and Petra paired up talking as they let Matt and Darrin ride ahead of them.

They had been riding for a while when they came across a grassy field with a worn trail leading towards a forested mountainside. Matt turned in his saddle to ask Casey and Petra if they were able to gallop. In their enthusiasm, they didn't even bother to answer but instead sped off past the boys who sat with their jaws dropped open in surprise. Nudging their horses into motion, they followed.

Casey was having so much fun that she didn't want to slow Storm down, but she decided that would be best as they came to the forest's edge. Matt and Darrin quickly caught up.

"Where did you learn to ride?" Darrin asked Casey.

"I do some riding back home every once in a while," she said. "I go to the local riding stables just outside of Edmonton. It's maybe a half-hour drive."

"Well, I think you're pretty good."

His remark made her blush—and once he realized what he had said, he squirmed a little.

Matt stepped in, trying to hide Darrin's embarrassment. "Why thank you, Darrin. You've never told me that before!"

Thankful for Matt's exceptional timing and humour, Darrin allowed himself to smile. "Well, you've never deserved it before!"

Petra moved her horse closer. "So where are we headed, Matt?"

"I found a nice place I wanted to show you guys. It's this way." With that, Matt turned his horse and followed the trail through the trees.

The conversation was light and humorous as they continued into a denser part of the forest. Petra and Casey rode together as Matt and Darrin took up the lead.

After they'd been riding for a while, Casey looked up and noticed that the sky was still overcast; it made the forest seem dark and claustrophobic. The ferns and evergreens converged, moss jutting out in patches to form their own trails amongst the rocks.

Matt pulled back on Napoleon's reins, causing him to stop.

"What do you think, Casey?" Petra asked, leaning forward in her saddle. "Is there something wrong?"

Puzzled, Casey watched as Matt and Darrin got into a heated conversation.

She nudged Storm forward to stand closer to the guys. "Hey, is everything all right?"

"No. Everything is not all right!" Darrin sounded quite perturbed.

"What's wrong, Matt?" Petra softly probed.

Matt was looking around with an uncertain expression. "It's just that... well, you know those last few turns we took? I think I may have taken a wrong one. But I was sure it was this way..."

"You mean you think we're lost?" Casey asked.

"Sorry. It's just kind of hard with so little sunlight today. If I knew we were heading west, I'd know we were on the right track."

"How about if I pray for an answer?" Casey suggested. "You can never go wrong with that. Plus, God knows where we are. He will lead us the right way... if we give Him the chance."

Matt and Petra nodded in agreement, although Darrin seemed sceptical.

"Go ahead if you want," said Darrin. "I know how well He answers prayer, but what have we got to lose? I guess this way for sure we'll find out if there really is a God. That is, if He can get us out of this mess."

Casey prayed, asking God for guidance to show them the way. And if it was His will, she asked that Darrin be shown that God really does care for us. She also asked that they have a great time exploring and not get too hungry before they got out of there.

"In Jesus' name, amen," she finally said, closing the prayer.

The three others lifted their heads up and opened their eyes to find Darrin staring at them.

"Well, I guess we might as well carry on," he said, moving Bandit ahead of them up the trail. "For the moment, there's not much else we can do."

Petra took off her fleece jacket and tied it around her waist. "Give Him a chance, Darrin. Jesus is always way more prepared than us."

"Whoa! Petra, put that jacket back on," Matt pleaded.

Darrin turned in his saddle to see what the commotion was about. Blinded by the sight of her fluorescent yellow shirt, even he couldn't help but laugh. "I'm sorry, Petra, but I'll have to agree with Matt on that one."

"Come on, you guys," said Petra. "If Pete was flying overtop and saw me, he could see us through the trees and…"

Darrin wasn't convinced. "If Pete were to fly overtop, he would never—"

They slowly looked up, following Darrin's lead, and at last saw the sun sending down rays through the treetops. Suddenly, right in front of them, a beam of sunshine lighted their trail.

Darrin looked at the trail and then back at them with a shocked look on his face.

"Well, what are you waiting for, Darrin?" Casey asked. "Let's check it out."

They nudged their horses into a trot, which quickly brought them out of the dense forest and into a beautiful meadow. The sun had broken through the clouds, revealing a picturesque view. To their left was a gorgeous waterfall with a small pool that spilt over into a creek which flowed down the mountain. The small meadow to their right was framed by the rocky mountainside and the spreading evergreen forest.

A flock of birds flew away, trying to find a hiding place amongst the foliage.

"Is this ever awesome!" Petra exclaimed.

Matt grinned. "Yeah. Is this a cool spot or what?"

"Or what!" Darrin, Casey, and Petra chimed together.

Laughing, Casey stopped to thank the Lord for His miracles.

Darrin walked Bandit over to her. "Well, I guess maybe He does listen to you. But I still don't think He hears me."

"He does hear you, though. Maybe He is waiting for you to trust Him." Casey tried to read his deep blue eyes, but all she could see was puzzlement and hurt.

*Heavenly Father, please open his heart and eyes to you.*

Darrin turned away, looking at Petra and Matt as they clowned around by the base of the waterfall.

"I guess we'd better go and look after those two before they fall in," Darrin remarked.

"Too late!" Casey answered as Matt sprawled backwards into the water with his arms flailing.

# Chapter Eight

They sat on the edge of the waterfall's pool and devoured the sandwiches and apples Matt had brought for them. Bandit was trying to sneak Darrin's apple away unnoticed, which didn't work.

"It's okay, Darrin," Matt whispered. "I brought an extra bag of apples for the horses. They're tucked in the other half of the saddlebags, if you want to grab them and feed Bandit."

As Darrin slowly got to his feet, Bandit walked over to where Napoleon was grazing peacefully.

Matt smiled broadly. "Now would you look at that! Sometimes I really wonder if that horse honestly knows what we're saying."

Amused, they all watched as Bandit started to sniff around the saddlebags.

"You better find them first before he wrecks the bags looking for them!" Matt yelled over to Darrin, who was trying to open the flap.

Victorious, Darrin pulled the bag of apples out and walked back towards the group with Bandit looking over his shoulder. He sat back down between Casey and Matt and retrieved a Swiss army knife from out of his back pocket. Cutting an apple into quarters, he shifted sideways to feed the pieces to Bandit.

"Maybe these pieces are easier to eat with the bridle on," Darrin murmured. "What do you think, Bandit?"

Bandit nodded and nudged Darrin in the back with such pressure that he nearly pushed Darrin over.

After watching this entertaining interaction, Petra got up to further explore their surroundings. "You know, Matt, this is a really nice spot. I mean, just look at the view. It's awesome! Next time, though, I think I'll bring my bathing suit and a towel."

"Good point!" Matt exclaimed as he wrung his shirt out; it was drying fast with all the sunshine and afternoon heat, but his blue jeans were still clinging wetly to his legs. Casey didn't even want to guess how squishy his sneakers must be. "I'll have to make a note."

Suddenly, Petra stopped and looked back at them. "Oh, I almost forgot!"

"What?" Casey asked.

"Make a note!"

Everyone looked at her in confusion, waiting for her explanation.

"It's the weirdest thing," Petra said. "You guys remember when I tried out the player piano yesterday and something seemed off? Well, I took those music sheets home last night and played them on my piano. One of the measures was different on the page than it was when the piano played it. I think I'd have to hear it again, but I think the piano played the wrong note."

Darrin wiped off his knife and stuffed it into his back pocket. "You found music sheets?"

"Yeah, and it's a beautiful song, *The Sweetheart's Melody*," said Petra wistfully. "So romantic. I didn't know your great-grandpa was such a talented composer, and to think he wrote it for his wife!"

Darrin choked on the piece of apple that he was eating. "What... are... you talking... about?" he sputtered. "What did you say that title was?"

By now he was starting to look a little pale.

"Darrin, are you okay?" Casey leaned over, ready to assist him if he needed first aid. She really hoped she wouldn't have to administer the abdominal thrust, for it had been a while since she had taken the course in health class.

Darrin shook his head but soon got his coughing under control and took a sip of water from the water bottle he had brought.

"I'm okay... it just freaked me out." He ran his fingers through his black hair. "Grandpa used to say all the time, 'The key is the sweetheart's song, Darrin my boy. Once you hear it, you'll recognize it.' I just thought he was thinking about Grandma, since he missed her so much after she passed away. Sometimes, when I was younger, I'd go over to visit them and Grandpa would be singing to her in the kitchen. I didn't think anything of it. Do you guys think he might have actually been talking about the song Great-Grandpa wrote?"

"Maybe," Petra said. "The music sheets say that a certain note should be a B-sharp, but the player piano played a B instead."

Matt was looking really confused. "What do you mean? A B-sharp is a B... isn't it?"

"No. A B-sharp doesn't exist. You would play the C key."

Darrin shook his head. "Now I'm confused, too."

"Thanks, man," Matt said, laughing. "At least now I know I'm not the only one."

Casey raised her hand. "Make it times three!" She turned to face Petra. "Can you explain it?"

"Sure! Let's see." Petra became quiet, contorting her lips as she thought of an easy way to put it. Biting her bottom lip, a smile suddenly came forth. "Okay, I think I've got it."

Jumping up, she walked to the edge of the meadow and returned with a twig in her hand.

"Oh no. She thinks she's a conductor now," Matt teased. "Forget it, I'm not going to sing. And that's final!"

Casey and Darrin laughed as Petra plunked herself down again and began to draw in the damp sand along the pool's bank. They all leaned in to watch as Petra sketched a series of piano keys.

"Okay, so if this was a piano, these keys here would be the white ones. And these other ones are the black keys."

They nodded their comprehension so far.

"On the music sheet, it says we should be playing these keys right here." Petra started to point at the keys with the stick. "F... then A... then a B-sharp, which is the white key here, as you would actually play a C. But I'm sure the tracker bar on the piano was playing this black key here, which is a B-flat. This doesn't make any sense."

"Ohhh," the rest of them replied in stereo.

Casey quickly turned to look at Darrin, who was leaning against her shoulder. "You don't think..." She shook her head. "Oh, never mind."

"Think what, Casey?" Darrin asked.

"Well, I was just wondering... what if Sir Edmond Masters did it on purpose?"

Now it was Petra's turn to look confused. "Did it on purpose? What do you mean?"

"It may just be a coincidence, but what if he was trying to tell your grandpa something... like, leave a clue behind?" Casey said. "Darrin, what if your grandpa was trying to let you know about it when he talked about 'the sweetheart's key.' Could this be clue to the so-called great treasure?"

Matt grabbed his head, pretending that he was starting to lose it. "Okay, I thought I was lost before, but now..."

"I'm with you on that one Matt." Darrin gazed back at Casey with a stumped look in his blue eyes.

"Casey is right. Let's go check it out!" Petra jumped up, knocking Casey off-balance so that she fell into Darrin. She rushed over to retrieve Gypsy from where she was grazing. "No one with a musical background would make this mistake, especially on such a personal song. I bet you he was trying to tell us something... maybe that we should *be sharp*?"

Scrambling to their feet, they went about catching their horses and mounting up. They cantered across the meadow and slowly re-entered the forest at a trot. Once they were through the woods, they galloped across the field to the dirt road that would lead them back to Matt's place.

Upon reaching the stable, everyone came to a halt as Matt slowed Napoleon.

"What do you think, Matt?" Darrin asked him.

Matt gently pulled the right rein, bringing Napoleon around so he could face the group. "If we use the horses, we can take the main road over to Mrs. B's place and cut down that trail. We could probably make pretty good time. Are you guys game?"

When they all nodded, he turned Napoleon and led them past his house and down the drive. In just a few moments they were stopping in front of Gran's store.

Casey kicked her feet out of the stirrups and slid off the saddle. "I'll just be a sec, guys. I want to tell Gran what's happening in case she sees us all fly past on the horses." She dashed inside and returned only a few moments later. She pulled herself back up into the saddle, then shortened the reins and came up alongside Gypsy. "It's all set, let's go!"

Nudging Storm into motion, she cantered across the field and down the trail.

They slowed the horses when the trail became a little rougher, letting them pick their way. And when they came to the end, they dismounted and led the horses through the brush.

Soon they were trotting down into the valley and approaching the main street. The town seemed to be deserted as they made their way towards the hotel. The weather was warming, too, with the sunshine reflecting off the windows.

Matt walked Napoleon around to the back of the hotel.

"Here's a great spot," he said, dismounting.

He wrapped Napoleon's reins around a rustic hitching post adjacent to the hotel's stable. Casey, Petra, and Darrin tied up their horses to the post right beside it. They made sure the horses would be okay in the shade, then entered through the hotel's back entrance.

The wooden floorboards creaked as they made their way into the dining room. Petra sat on the piano bench.

"Here goes!" She placed her feet on the pedals and pumped. The music roll started to turn and the keys moved. The lulling melody filled the air and for a moment they all seemed to forget why they were there.

Observing the notes being played, Petra quickly got them to focus their attention.

"Okay, this is it here!" She pointed out the keys. "And… see it played a B-flat instead of a C."

She stopped pumping the pedals and turned to look at them.

"Petra, why don't you try playing it the way the music sheet says?" Casey asked. She wasn't sure what to expect, but she watched as Petra positioned her fingers on the keys.

A moment later, the tune was once again echoing through the empty dining room.

As Petra touched the C, they all suddenly heard a strange sound emanating from somewhere inside the piano.

"Hey, what was that?" Matt asked.

"I'm not sure," Petra replied. "Hold on. I'll try the song again."

She played the same section of the melody—and when it came time to press down on the C key again, they all heard the same sound.

Casey leaned in closer to the piano. Excitement filled her voice. "Hey you guys, check this out."

Reaching for the woodwork on the front of the piano, she gingerly touched one of the intricately carved hummingbirds that was retrieving nectar from a flower. The bird slowly opened away from the piano, as if on a hinge of some sort. As it moved, a small piece of paper fluttered down onto the keys.

Matt let out a low sounding whistle between his pursed lips. "What does it say?"

Casey picked up the textured piece of paper—once white, but since yellowed with age—and carefully unfolded it. There was only one fold, across the middle. The black ink stood out:

*Have you forgotten to tip the waiter?*

"Have you forgotten to tip the waiter? What is that supposed to mean?" Matt blurted out.

Darrin seemed just as puzzled. "I don't know. Maybe the waiter put it there?"

Petra started to giggle. "Maybe the note was left for you, Matt! Have you tipped your waiter recently? Maybe Mabel put it there just for you."

Casey sat down at one of the nearby tables and stared at the note. Just what was it supposed to mean? It had to have some purpose for someone to have gone to all that trouble to put it in there.

She glanced over to her friends. "Just how did this note get in there?"

"Good question." Petra turned around on the piano seat and faced the keys again. "Well, if Mr. Masters had the music roll made specifically that it wouldn't play the C, perhaps that opens it somehow."

"Yeah," Matt said, "but anyone playing the piano could have hit that key and unlocked the bird at any time, right?"

Darrin brushed the top of the piano. "Maybe we should take a look inside it. Help me lift the lid, Matt."

With one on each side of the piano, they slowly lifted the heavy wooden top. Casey and Petra looked into the piano, trying to see if they could spot something out of the ordinary.

Petra was the first to spot it. "Right there," she said, pointing.

"What do you see?" Matt squinted, trying to see what she was pointing at.

"There's a line of some sort attached to the two keys. I bet that the arm attached to the hammer pulls that line when A and C keys are pressed in sequence," Petra said. "It tightens through here and pops this little mechanism, unlatching the hummingbird."

She followed the line with her finger, then sat down and put her fingers back on the piano keys.

"Watch."

Petra began to play the piano as Matt, Casey, and Darrin watched the strings move. When she got to the sequence in question and pressed the A and C keys, the line tightened and the hummingbird once again engaged.

"Hey, that's pretty sneaky," Matt said, chuckling.

Darrin reached in and touched the line to confirm his suspicions. "Yeah, you noticed it too?"

"Noticed what?" Casey gave them a quizzical expression.

"They rigged it using the old linen-style fishing line so it wouldn't be as easily spotted if someone just happened to look inside the piano," Matt said.

"Plus that fishing line is pretty strong and durable," added Darrin.

A floorboard up above them creaked and tiny dust particles floated down from the ceiling. The group became very silent and looked up. Petra gasped at the sound of light footsteps crossing the room above them.

"There's someone here," Petra squeaked, terrified.

Darrin motioned towards the hallway. "Hey, Matt, let's check it out."

"No problem. Let's go." Matt touched Petra on her shoulder. "You and Casey stay here. We'll be right back."

Casey grinned at them. "And if you scream, we'll come and rescue you guys."

Matt and Darrin took off as quietly as they could.

Straining to hear, Casey closed her eyes and followed their path in her mind, imagining them taking steps as the floorboards groaned occasionally from them shifting their weight on loose boards. Before long, she could hear the shuffling of feet just above them.

"I'm sorry, Petra, but I have to go," Casey said. "The curiosity is killing me."

Petra sighed and got up from the piano bench. "It's okay... but I'm going with you."

She glued herself next to Casey as they vacated the dining room. Petra's black hair bopped in its ponytail as she looked nervously about. They started to ascend the staircase, taking extra care to step around the ones that were obviously loose.

They were halfway up when Casey heard the building's back door faintly close. Placing her hand on Petra's arm, she stopped and listened. Instantly making up her mind, Casey turned and raced down the stairs. She ran through the hallway and kitchen, then flung the back door open and looked outside.

Petra clambered out behind Casey and bumped into her.

"What is it, Casey?" she whispered, tickling her friend's ear. "Do you see something?"

Giggling, Casey brushed her ear and looked back at Petra. "Hey, that tickles!"

"Sorry!"

"That's okay." Shrugging her shoulders, Casey turned to go back inside. "I can't see anything out here. Let's go see if the guys found something."

They closed the door and headed back towards the main staircase. Matt and Darrin were just coming back down.

Matt was the first to speak. "Nothing up there."

"There were some marks near the window in the bedroom, though," Darrin informed them. "But they looked like they were made by a raccoon."

"And that was all that you found?" Casey asked.

"Why, what's up?" Darrin moved towards them. "Are you guys okay?"

"Casey heard something and ran out the back door." Petra pulled her fleece jacket back on, trying to cover up her goosebumps.

Matt seemed bewildered. "Really? What did you hear?"

"I guess it was nothing... I mean, I didn't see anything... so..."

"But you thought you did hear something?" Darrin prompted.

"Yeah. I thought that I heard the back door close. I don't know... I guess maybe it was just my imagination."

Petra smiled reassuringly. "It's okay, Casey."

"Yeah, don't worry." Matt started towards the door, "Anyway, I guess we should head back to the house and get the horses cleaned up. My shift at the store starts at 3:00 and Dylan will be expecting me. He has a dinner date with his girlfriend Jenny lined up, so he'll really have my hide if I'm late."

Glancing at her watch, Casey was surprised to see that it was already 2:15. "We'd better get a move on then."

They closed the door behind them, untied the horses, mounted them, and then nudged them into motion.

Upon returning to the stable, they removed and cleaned the tack and put it away. Once they'd given the horses a good brushing, Matt let the horses loose to roam the pasture.

"So do you guys want to go to the late movie tonight?" Darrin asked as they walked up to his dirt bike. "There's supposed to be a comedy playing."

Looking back and forth, they all nodded one by one.

"Sounds good to me." Matt picked up a stray bucket and hung it on an empty hook. "I'll be closing up shop at 6:00, so it'll give me time to grab a quick bite before we meet." He turned to Casey. "Do you want me to stop by and pick you up on the quad? If it's okay with Petra, we could all meet at her house."

Petra nodded as she retrieved her mountain bike, which had been leaning against a tree. "What time do you guys want to meet?"

"Let's say 7:30," said Darrin. "Just in time to catch the 8:00 show."

Once they'd made their plan, Darrin pulled his bike away from the fence and straddled it. He put his helmet on.

"I'll see you guys later then," he said as he kicked over the starter level and revved the bike.

He released the brakes, gave the engine some gas, then edged the bike around the gate as Matt held it open. They all watched as he waved goodbye and roared off.

Casey and Petra said goodbye to Matt, then began the walk across the beach back towards Gran's house.

"Do you really think you heard that door close?" Petra asked.

"Yeah… I just really wished I had seen who it was."

Petra thought about it. "I wonder if that means someone overheard what we said about the piano?"

"Possibly."

Before long, Petra got on her bike and pedalled away. Casey watched her disappear into the distance, then walked into the store. She dodged the door chimes as she entered and glanced towards Gran, who was standing behind the counter.

*Ghost towns, moving hummingbirds, anonymous visitors…* She shook her head, trying to rid herself of the cobwebs in it. *This is getting crazy.*

Right then and there, she decided that what she needed was a cold glass of iced tea.

# Chapter Nine

As Gran and Casey rode into town in the pickup truck, music playing loudly over the radio, Casey looked down the road towards Crystal Creek. It was a perfect morning, the sun shining through the sparse clouds scattered across the blue sky. She relaxed her arm on the windowsill and enjoyed the fresh breeze as it flowed through the cab.

"So there wasn't anyone there when you looked?" Gran asked.

"Nope." Casey couldn't hide the frustration in her voice. "You know, Gran, if only I had been a little quicker, I may have caught a glimpse of who it was. But—"

"Well now, Cassandra, I'm sure it had nothing to do with your agility. It sounds like they had a headstart, that's all. The question is, how did they become aware that you guys were on to them?"

"I thought about that. We probably tipped them off when we got quiet in the dining room."

"How do you think they got past you guys on the stairs? You said the boys had already headed up there when you and Petra followed."

"I think they stole down the hallway and crept down the servants' staircase when they heard the boys coming up. That's how they got to the back door without passing us. Plus, the guys were distracting me and I was trying to focus on whether or not someone was going to come down the main staircase. I really hadn't thought about anyone using the back stairs. Like, those stairs are so narrow and steep. I couldn't picture anyone coming down them in a hurry."

Gran smiled at her. "Well. when I was your age…"

Casey laughed. "I'm sorry, Gran. Yeah, I guess a lot of houses had tiny staircases back then, right?"

"It was mostly the back stairs in those days. The main stairs were always made to look elegant and majestic." Gran pulled into the parking lot of Sam's Food Store. "So you're okay with picking up the mail for me?"

Casey nodded as they got out of the truck. "Yeah. I mean, yes, it's no problem. I'll find you inside the store."

"Okay, here's the key." Gran placed the key in Casey's open hand, then pointed down the street. "The post office is just around that corner and down two blocks. You'll find it on the righthand side, next to the bookstore."

"See you in a few."

Casey started to cross the parking lot. As she strode along, she fell into deep thought, pondering the mystery at hand.

*Meep-meep.*

At the sound of the horn, Casey jumped and moved away from the edge of the sidewalk. She glanced to her left just as Matt pulled up alongside her with the quad.

"What's up?" she asked, grinning.

Turning the key on the quad, Matt pulled off his helmet and brushed the top of his hair with the palm of his hand. "Not much. I'm just doing the mail run today. You?"

"Same."

They walked together for a while. When they got to the post office, she pulled the door open and Matt held it for her.

She retrieved the mail from its locked box, then walked over to the small table by the entrance. She spread the mail over the tabletop, sifting through it to see if anything had come for her.

She spotted a package with her name on it, then took note of the sender and the return address. Her parents' boss had mailed it.

Matt came up beside her. "What have you got there?"

Casey shrugged her shoulders. "Not sure yet. Have you got a knife on you?"

He nodded and handed her the pocketknife he had been carrying in his jeans.

As he watched, she proceeded to open the package. Three items fell out—a small handwritten note, a letter from her parents, and a little box. She started with the note:

Miss Blake:

Just wanted to let you know that your parents are doing well. I was able to meet with them on Friday before my flight home from Geneva. They knew I was headed back to Vancouver for a meeting, so they asked me to do this small favour for them. Of course I couldn't refuse and that's why you're reading this. They wanted you to receive this package as soon as possible, otherwise they would have sent it themselves.

I do apologize for the interruption in your summer plans, Casey. I hope you'll be able to forgive me.

Anyway, if you need anything, you know how to get a hold of me. Shannon can always patch you through.

Yours truly,
Mr. George McCleod

P.S. See you at Christmas dinner again?

"Isn't that your parents' boss?" Matt asked.

She nodded and excitedly opened her parents' letter, which she quickly read.

"They're doing great but miss me," she summarized after scanning it. "And Mom found something she thought was cute. They've sent it over."

Casey picked up the little box, cut through the tape, and lifted the lid. Inside she found a gold chain with a charm hanging from it. Taking the chain out of the box, she discovered that it was a necklace with a miniature golden cowbell. As she gently shook the bell, it emitted a tinkling sound. Her face lit up with pleasure.

"Would you like me to help you put it on?" Matt asked.

"Yes, please."

Once they'd retrieved their mail, Casey and Matt strolled outside and met Petra just as she was walking by the doors of the post office.

"Hello there!" Petra said. "Isn't it a wonderful day out?"

"Yup!" Matt checked Petra out with one of his eyebrows raised. "So what are you up to now?"

"Nothing much. Hey, that's a pretty necklace, Casey." Petra reached forward and daintily touched the cowbell, which tinkled.

Casey smiled. "Isn't it! Mom and Dad just sent it over from Geneva."

Petra motioned towards the bookstore behind her. "I was just going to take a look in there and see if there was anything new. Do you guys want to come in with me?"

Matt and Casey joined her as she went inside. Casey looked around at all the freestanding bookshelves laden with both paperbacks and hardcovers. The smell of old and new books mingled in the air.

She found the geography section and located a small paperback about Switzerland. Flipping through its pages and glancing at the pictures, Casey started to get the eerie feeling that someone was watching her.

She put the book back on the shelf and went in search of Petra and Matt. Walking towards the back of the store, she peered down each aisle. Halfway to the back of the store, she heard voices and made a beeline for them.

As she turned to pass between the shelves, she glanced behind her and saw the figure of the woman who had been at The Malt Junction on Sunday. The woman quickly disappeared into the geography section.

"Matt! Petra!" she whispered. "Pssst. Come here!"

Petra replaced the book she had been looking at and walked over to her. "Is everything okay?"

"There's a woman here that I saw at The Malt Junction."

"Well, this *is* a small town," Matt teased.

Casey made her way along a corridor that ran parallel to the store's interior wall. "I know that, Matt, but I have this feeling that this lady is following us."

"Really?" Petra sounded surprised. "What did she look like?"

Casey searched the area where she had seen the woman, but suddenly she heard the door chimes as the front door closed. Darting out into the open, she caught a glimpse of the hem of a woman's dress vanishing around the corner of the building.

She ran outside, determined not to let the woman get away before she could find out why they were being followed. Rounding the store, she spotted the figure in the dress.

"Wait!" she called.

Casey caught up, then stopped to catch her breath as Matt and Petra joined her. Casey straightened and stared into the woman's hazel eyes.

She groaned. "I'm sorry. Wrong person…"

The woman smiled and dropped a pair of sunglasses over her eyes. "That's okay, dear."

"Sorry about that, Mrs. Peterson," Petra said.

The woman carried on.

Casey looked sheepishly at her friends. "Sorry, guys. She had the same dress. I thought it was her."

"You mean the right woman might still be in the store?" Matt asked. He immediately started back the way they had come.

After they had searched the store with no results, they met up outside again.

Casey sat down on the edge of the sidewalk, shaking her head. "She must have slipped out while we were chasing the other one."

"Sorry, Casey," Matt said. "There aren't a lot of clothing stores here, so occasionally people end up wearing identical clothing."

"Tell me about it," Petra grumbled. "That's why I love when we go to the city. Especially before school starts."

"Well, maybe next time. Except next time that I see her, I'll make sure I stop her and find out if it's just all a coincidence." Casey got up, brushing off her pants. "But for now I should be getting back to Gran. She had to do some grocery shopping and I was supposed to meet up with her there."

"Yeah, I have to get back too," Matt said. "Mom's expecting me."

After placing his mail into the knapsack, he pulled on his helmet, started the quad, and waved goodbye.

Casey and Petra turned and started up the street towards the grocery store.

"It's okay, Casey," said Petra, trying to cheer her up. "This town is so small that I'm sure you'll bump into whoever it was again."

"Thanks Petra."

As they rounded the block, Casey heard some noise down the road from the store. "What's going on down there?"

"Oh, I forgot to tell you. The fair pulled in this morning," Petra said excitedly. "They should be set up by tonight. Did you want to check it out?"

"Sure!" The excitement was becoming contagious as a plan started to form in Casey's mind. "I could stop by Essentially Barnetts later this afternoon to see if Matt wants to go with us."

"Could you?" Petra shyly asked. Then she suddenly clapped her hands together. "and if you want, I could mention it to Darrin on my way home. I have to stop by his family's hardware store to pick up a couple of things for my dad."

Casey smiled. "Sounds like a deal. Call you later?"

"I'll be waiting!"

Petra said goodbye and carried on her journey.

Casey entered the air-conditioned grocery store and walked past the shopping carts on her search for Gran. She finally located her in the produce section. Gran was bagging some oranges.

"Hi, Gran." She placed the mail into the seat of the cart. "Did you need a hand?"

"That would be nice, Cassandra." Gran opened her shopping list and ran her finger down each item on it. "Could you find me six bags of hot dog buns for the store, please?"

"Sure thing. I'll be right back."

She quickly found the buns and returned with them. Placing them in the shopping cart, she leaned over Gran's shoulder to see what else was on the list. Gran had ticked them off as she went. The only item remaining: marshmallows.

"Just one more thing and I'm done." Gran pushed the cart over to the next aisle. Finding the marshmallows, she retrieved four bags and placed them with the rest of the groceries. "So I see that you found the post office without difficulty?"

Nodding, Casey pushed the cart towards the till with the smallest line-up. "I got a package from Mom and Dad. See what they sent me?"

She lifted the chain off her shirt so Gran could see.

"Well, isn't that pretty. Does the bell work?"

Casey demonstrated. The air around them quickly filled with the tinkling chime.

"Is that ever cute!" commented the young brunette cashier who was busy scanning their purchases. "Where did you get it from?"

"My parents just sent it from Geneva," Casey felt a little embarrassed, not having realized that she had caught more than just her grandmother's attention. She let the chain fall back onto her T-shirt.

"Well, it's a very pretty charm." The cashier smiled and continued working. "So Mrs. Blake, how's the store coming along?"

Casey listened to them talk and then helped Gran take the groceries out to the truck. While she was loading them into the back, they both heard the sounds of a fair coming from further up the street.

"Is it that time of year again?" Gran asked. She had finished placing the last bag in the back.

"Yeah. I ran into Petra and Matt while I was getting the mail and Petra mentioned that the fair was here. Would it be okay with you if I hung out with them tonight and go check out the rides?"

"Sure. It'll give me a chance to visit with my friends at the Lodge. Some of them wanted to go bowling tonight. Maybe we'll bump into each other, being in the same neighbourhood."

"Awesome!" Casey flashed her a smile and went to return the shopping cart as Gran started up the truck.

Gran soon pulled the truck up alongside her and Casey jumped in.

"Well, if we're both going out tonight, I guess we'd better get back so I can get some things done," Gran said as she drove out of the parking lot and headed south.

During the ride, Casey read out loud the note she'd gotten from Mr. McCleod and the letter from her parents.

In a very short time, they had cleaned out the truck and put away all the groceries. Gran then went straight to preparing a light lunch as Casey ran upstairs to put away her mail. She quickly changed into a pair of shorts and brushed her hair back into a ponytail, which she tied back as she descended the staircase.

Gran was just placing a plate of egg salad sandwiches on the table when Casey entered.

"I'll be in the store if you need me later," Gran said after saying grace. "What time would you like to have supper?"

"Actually, if it's okay with you, I thought I'd try to make you spaghetti tonight?"

Gran gave her a warm smile. "Now that would be very nice, Cassandra. I'd love to have some spaghetti."

"Good! Then it's settled. Supper at, say... 5:00?"

"Sounds perfect."

Finishing her sandwich, Gran went and placed her dirty dish into the sink.

Casey quickly followed. "I'm just going to run over and see Matt for a second and then I'll be back, okay?"

"That's fine with me, dear. I'm going to put my feet up before I get back to work."

"Okay. I'll be right back. And then, Gran...?"

At the sound of the sudden change of tone in Casey's voice, Gran turned and gave her a concerned expression. "Is everything okay, Cassandra?"

"Oh, yeah. It's just that I was going to wash some clothes... if you'll show me how the machine works."

"Of course, dear, I'd be happy to. Now go and see Matt. I'll show you before I leave to open the store."

Casey gave her grandmother a hug and then ran out the door. She soon found that jogging along the shoreline was a lot easier than struggling with the loose sand on the beach.

She made good time and was soon climbing up the dock and entering Essentially Barnetts. Fishing tackle and nets lined the right-hand wall while a souvenir line of clothing occupied the left. Between them were racks with lifejackets and canoe and kayak paddles.

Casey made her way to the front of the store, searching the faces of customers until she noticed Matt's brother Dylan sitting behind the front counter.

She strode up to the counter. "You must be Dylan, Matt's brother. Is he around?"

"Hey, Casey. Matt told me all about you." Dylan smiled. "Matt's outside filling up the Grumman Goose."

"Thanks!"

In a flash, she was out the front doors and walking down the dock towards the plane, where Matt was standing next to his Uncle Pete.

Matt spotted her coming. "How's it going, Casey?"

"Matt. I see you're keeping busy."

"You bet. Casey, this is my Uncle Pete. Uncle Pete, this is Casey, Mrs. B's granddaughter."

She extended her hand to him. "Nice to meet you, Pete."

Pete was really cute, especially with his dimples. Casey guessed he must be around twenty-seven or twenty-eight—and a perfect match for her Auntie Natasha, she thought.

Pete started to smirk as he seemed to realize that the girl before him had the look of someone with a scheme developing in her sparkling blue eyes.

"Nice to meet ya, Casey."

Casey brushed her bangs out of her eyes. Remembering why she was there, she turned to face Matt. "I just came by to see if you wanted to meet up later and head into town. The fair has arrived!"

"Oh... sure!"

"And Petra will be there, too."

"Really?" The tone of his voice betrayed his thoughts and confirmed Casey's suspicions.

"Yup, and she was hoping you could come."

"Really?"

"And I told her it was no problem, since I was sure you would try to make it."

"Really?"

Pete tapped Matt on the shoulder, trying to snap him out of it.

"I'm sure he can, Casey," Pete replied with a grin.

"Huh?" Matt brightened. "Oh, yeah. Most definitely!"

"I'll let her know then," Casey said. "Pop over to the house before you go and we can walk together."

"Or I could bring the quad?"

"Or you could bring the quad." She started to turn away. "See ya later. Bye, Pete."

"See ya, Casey," Matt and Pete chimed in at the same time.

Casey shook her head and smiled as she descended the stairs to the right of the store. Within a few minutes she'd returned to the house and got started on some laundry. She started by going through the hamper in her room, sorting the clothes into piles.

Gran entered. "While you were out, Petra called and said she talked to Darrin. Tonight is a go. How did things go with Matthew?"

"He said he'd stop by on his way to town," Casey explained. "That way we can double on his quad again."

She struggled to pick up some of her laundry and headed out into the hallway with her load. As she started toward the stairs, though, she heard Gran following right behind her.

"What are you doing, Cassandra?"

Bewildered, she slowly turned. "I was taking my laundry downstairs!"

"Come here. I want to show you something."

Casey followed Gran halfway down the upstairs hallway. "What is it, Gran?"

Gran reached forward and placed her hands on a wooden panel on the wall. She pushed up on it and the panel moved, disappearing from Casey's view. Right before them was another square panel with a latch.

"Whoa, what's that?" Casey asked.

"It's the easy way."

Casey stepped forward and inspected the space. Undoing the latch, she hesitantly slid the board up and found that it was a door of some sort. She stuck her head inside the wooden box and looked around.

Bringing her head back out, she looked at Gran for an explanation.

"You put your laundry in here and then we transfer it to the first floor," Gran turned and headed for the stairs, calling over her shoulder, "Just put it in and close the door. I'll meet you downstairs."

Casey looked at the pile of clothes on the floor, then shrugged and placed the clothes inside. She closed the door and headed down to the laundry room.

Coming around the corner, she saw her grandma now taking her clothes out of the contraption.

"So what is this thing?" Casey asked.

"Isn't it awesome? The best invention, I think. Every house should have one. It's too bad they don't usually build them anymore."

Gran slid the wall panel back into place.

Casey took a closer look at the wall. "You can't really see it! How did you even know it was there?"

"A woman always knows where to find the dumbwaiter."

"Oh." The comment struck a chord. "The what?"

"The dumbwaiter." She glanced at Casey as she carried the clothes over to the laundry room. "Cassandra, are you all right?"

"That's gotta be it, Gran!"

# Chapter Ten

C asey started to dance around in a circle. Gran watched her with a look on her face that made Casey think she was convinced her granddaughter had lost her mind.

"Cassandra, honey, please tell me you're okay. You can't have heatstroke since you weren't outside that long…"

Casey ran over to Gran and gave her a big hug, laundry and all. "Thanks, Gran! You're awesome. You just solved the clue. I'm sure of it!"

"The clue?" Gran shook her head as she dropped the load of dirty clothes onto the small table beside the washer. Placing her hands onto her hips, she looked to Casey for an explanation.

"Remember? I told you about that note we found, locked behind the hummingbird and the carvings on the piano."

A pensive look crossed Gran's features. "Oh yes. Now I remember… something about a waiter, you said."

Gran sorted the clothes into a load of whites and a load of colours. Depositing the whites inside of the washer, she turned on the machine and added the soap before she closed the lid.

"What did the note say again?" she asked.

"'Have you forgotten to tip the waiter?'"

Once Gran was finished, they walked into the living room. Casey sat down on the couch while Gran chose the rocker next to the fireplace.

"So what do you think it means, Cassandra? The note is a little vague."

"I have a feeling that Edmond Masters put it there to remind someone to check the dumbwaiter in case they had forgotten about it."

"Hmmm. That could be! What do you think is in the dumbwaiter?"

Casey frowned, feeling stumped. "I'm not really sure."

"Oh, and another thing is… which dumbwaiter?"

"Pardon?"

Gran just kept rocking in her chair. "Well, with a house this big, I have two dumbwaiters. So…"

"Wow!" Casey started to look around the house more closely. "You mean that since it's a hotel, there may be more than one…"

"Precisely." Gran got up and went down the hallway to check on the laundry.

Casey trailed behind her grandmother, pausing in the hallway to stare at the concealed dumbwaiter. *More than one! How are we going to find them all?*

"How would we find a dumbwaiter if we don't know where they are?" Casey asked.

Tossing the wet clothes into the dryer, Gran started the next load. "Well, you could check some of the more obvious places… like Edmond's own suite. You could also check the hallways, or look around near the servants' staircase." She tilted her head in thought. "And maybe if you tap the walls, you could find spots where the wood sounds different… that might indicate that something's there. It's hard to say, though, since things were made to last back then. The wood should be pretty solid. But just pray for God to help you and I'm sure you'll find what you're looking for in no time flat!"

Feeling more determined than ever, Casey nodded. "If Matt, Darrin, and Petra are with me, we'll have the whole place checked fast. With God on our side, we'll find it."

Gran put her arm around Casey's shoulders and gave them a squeeze. "Now that's my granddaughter!" She glanced at her watch. "But I have to get going. You'll be okay. All you have to do is fold the laundry that's in the dryer when it's done. Then put the next load in and turn it on."

Casey reassured her that everything was under control; if she had a problem, all she had to do was pop over to the store and ask.

With that, Casey went up to her room. Going through her backpack, she found a pen and a pad of paper. She returned to the couch, made herself comfortable, and started to write a letter to her mom and dad. When she was finished, she folded the paper and stuck it in an envelope that she retrieved from one of the drawers in the kitchen. After sealing it, she went to finish the laundry.

The old clock in the living room soon filled the quiet house with its deep, striking bongs. Casey's eyes searched for Gran out the kitchen window and saw her on her way back to the house.

Crossing over to the stove, Casey picked up the bowl of spaghetti she had made and placed it on the table beside Gran's plate. The porch door opened and soon Gran was in the kitchen washing her hands over the sink.

Gran smiled at Casey. "Mmmmm, it sure smells good! Looks good too."

Using the oven mitts, Casey placed the warm pot of spaghetti sauce on the cutting board and transferred it to the table.

"Supper is served," she said as she took the mitts off and sat down.

Gran brought the cold jug of milk from the fridge. "Would you like to say grace, Cassandra?"

They bowed their heads as Casey started.

"Dear heavenly Father, thank You so much for all You have given us—the food, the friends, and of course our family. Thank You also for the time we can share together. Please be with Mom and Dad, and please be with us as we go out tonight. In Jesus' name I pray, amen."

After they had finished eating, Gran helped to clean off the table.

"Dear, if I'm still in town when you come home, and you want to go out again, just use this notepad to write down where you're going." Gran pushed the pad towards Casey. "And if I go somewhere else, I'll leave you a note, okay?"

"No problem. What time do you want me back at?"

"Can I call you Cinderella?"

Casey grinned at her grandmother. "Sounds good to me!"

She heard the sound of a quad approaching and ran to the washroom to freshen up. When she returned to the kitchen, she gave Gran a hug and started to put on her shoes.

"Here, Cassandra."

Looking up, Casey saw that Gran had placed some money on the counter for her.

"I know rides aren't free," Gran said. "Plus, if you want to grab a bite while you're there…"

"Thanks, Gran." She gave her grandmother a kiss on the cheek and ran outside to meet up with Matt.

"Hey, Matt. How's it going?"

"Awesome! Isn't this weather just perfect?" He handed Casey the extra helmet as she jumped onto the back of the quad.

They made it to town in no time at all. Before long they came to Petra's home, a beautiful three-storey brick house with cedar shingles. Matt drove up beside the garage and parked the quad in the back.

As Casey climbed off and removed the helmet, Petra came out of the house to welcome them.

"Glad you could make it," Petra said. "Ready to get going?"

Together, the three of them cut through the backyard and headed down the alley.

"We're supposed to meet Darrin over at The Light House," Petra explained. "He said that would be quicker than stopping by his place. So I gave him a call when I heard you guys pull up. He's already heading over there."

"Is the fair pretty big?" Casey asked.

Matt grinned at her. "It's nothing like you'd expect, this being such a small town and all. Just wait and see!"

"It's pretty amazing, Casey." In Petra's excitement, she picked up her pace. "I can smell the popcorn from here."

Not willing to straggle behind, Casey and Matt hurried to catch up.

They all jogged past Sam's Food Store, and before Casey knew it they were slowing to a stop in front of The Light House. Darrin stood out front waiting for them, leaning against the picket fence. Seeing them, he moved forward and joined them on the road.

"Hey guys! Ya ready for this?"

Sprawled before them was quite the fair. It was so big that Casey couldn't fathom where it ended. The aromas of hot dogs, popcorn, and mini donuts invaded her senses, making her mouth water even though she had just eaten supper. As she stood there gawking, people of all ages streamed past her, coming and going from all the activities.

Suddenly, lights started flashing to the right of her as they made their way to the ticket booth.

"You're right," Casey said in awe. "For a small town, this *is* really big!"

The rest of them smiled at her. She didn't even know where to start; to her, it was like a sensory overload.

"Do you guys want to start with the games first?" Matt asked.

Petra moved over to stand next to Casey. "I'll just watch. I'm not that good with these games."

"It's okay, neither am I," Casey assured her. "I'll hang out with you as we watch the guys."

"In that case, I'll win you a stuffy," Matt boasted.

Darrin smiled. "Well then, to make things fair, I'll win toys for Casey."

The guys looked at each other with the biggest grins Casey had ever seen, and she knew the games were about to meet their match.

The girls cheered on the boys as they strolled from one game to the next, including the ring toss, the fish pond, and the rising waters. The games tested their strength and skill with darts, baseballs, rings, and of course the gigantic sledgehammer.

*Ding.* Matt put the hammer down and did a victory dance when he managed to ring the bell and win a prize. Petra giggled as he tried to stuff another toy into her arms.

Next, Darrin walked up to the contraption and picked up the hammer. He eyed the bell at the top, then slowly raised the hammer over his head and then, with force, hit the pad. The button swiftly rose to ring the bell at the top.

"Aha!" he cheered.

Picking out a little black-and-white stuffed cow, he gave it to Casey.

Darrin smiled. "Just something to go with your cowbell necklace."

Casey looked down at the cowbell. "Oh! Mom and Dad just sent it to me from Geneva."

"Does it work?"

She picked it up and jiggled it. The tinkling from the cowbell filled the air around them.

"Hmm, I'm impressed," Darrin said.

"Thanks!" She reached out and touched his arm. "And thanks for the cow."

Darrin started to mumble something, feeling embarrassed. Then he turned to the others. "Hey, do you guys want to go on some of the rides?"

They walked over to one that was called the Inverter. The machine was turning people upside-down.

Petra held onto her stuffed toys tighter, "Is it okay if I go onto the carousel instead?"

"I'll go with you," Casey said, motioning to her. "The guys can meet up with us near the rollercoaster later."

Matt and Darrin glanced at each other, then quickly made off towards the Inverter.

When the girls got to the carousel, Casey chose an elegant white horse with an ornate saddle. Casey shifted her toys around, enabling her to get on. Once she was settled in the saddle, she moved the toys around again so she'd be able to hang on without dropping any.

Petra picked the pure black horse beside her. After struggling with her arms full, she got herself positioned just as the controller for the ride started to walk by. He had to make sure she wasn't going to fall off if he started the machine.

"I can't believe I'm so embarrassed about holding so many stuffed toys," Petra remarked, blushing profusely.

Casey laughed. "I can't believe Matt won so many for you!"

"I *know!*"

The music on the carousel started to play and the ride slowly turned, picking up speed as it went.

Feeling festive afterward, they found the guys waiting for them by the rollercoaster. Then they tried the bumper cars and something the guys called the "drop of fear." Only Matt and Darrin went on that one.

While they were waiting for the guys to finish, Casey and Petra stopped by one of the concession stands. Casey couldn't resist buying a bag of pink and blue cotton candy; Petra opted for a candy apple and blueberry-flavoured snow cone. They found a bench to sit on and enjoy the treats.

Biting off a piece of cotton candy, Casey took in the action all around her. She enjoyed listening to the laughter and screams, the mechanical noises from the rides, and the operators calling out from their booths. Casey tried to absorb it all.

"Casey, the guys are back!"

Casey followed Petra's gaze to see the guys walking back towards them with big smiles on their faces.

"Did either of you want to go on the Ferris wheel?" Matt asked.

Petra smiled shyly. "That would be nice."

Petra ended up being the first one in line. The operator led her and Matt to an empty seat and latched them in. Next, Casey found herself sharing a seat with Darrin. The bar came over their heads and locked them in together.

Sitting quietly beside him, she took in the sights below as the Ferris wheel started to turn. She felt a sense of calm amidst the noise, relaxing in the seat and enjoying the view of the town.

Darrin glanced around nervously, his eyes finally settling on hers. "So what you said about trusting Him... is it true?" he quietly asked.

"Yes. Have you ever thought of talking to Him about your grandpa?"

Pain crossed his features as the muscles in his jaws tensed. "No."

With that, Darrin looked back towards the crowds below.

"Did you know that He knew what our sins would be even before He died for us?" Casey asked, her soft voice breaking the silence between them.

"Did He know that I would blame Him for my grandfather's death?"

"Yes… and Darrin?" Casey silently prayed for the hurt and confusion he was going through. If only he could understand…

"Yeah?"

"He still loves you. And no matter what you've done, His arms are always open… waiting for you to trust in Him. Believe in Him and ask for Him to forgive you for what you've done. Don't forget that He already knows what we've done and yet He still died for us. I think that's pretty awesome!"

"But is it really that easy?"

"Yeah. Darrin, what you have to remember is that none of us in this world are worthy of Him. It is because God loved us so much that He sent His Son Jesus to die on the cross for us so we could have everlasting life. All we have to do is believe that He died for us and rose again. You have to trust in Him."

As the ride stopped and they waited for their seat to be let down and unlocked, Casey looked into his eyes, trying to see if her words were making any sense to him. Noticing the pensive look on his face, Casey didn't push. If it was part of God's plan, it would happen in God's timing; she had nothing to do with it.

The operator lifted the bar, letting Casey and Darrin rejoin Matt and Petra.

"Hey, do you two want to go over to The Malt Junction for something to eat?" Matt asked.

His stomach growled—and they all knew it was serious when they realized how loud his stomach must be in order to be heard above all the noise.

Laughing, they walked the four blocks to the diner. They passed many people headed in the opposite direction, but it only took a few minutes to get there. They arrived just in time, because Matt's stomach protested yet again.

"Boy, Matt, didn't you eat anything for supper?" teased Darrin.

He had just finished his sentence when his own stomach let out a roar.

"Oh no, not a growling contest!" Petra said, smiling as Amanda came over to their table with menus.

Amanda must have overheard her. "A growling contest? Not in here! And don't forget, I can kick you out if you misbehave!"

Matt looked first to Darrin, then back towards his sister. "Aww, come on."

"No! And that's final." Amanda smiled. "I'll be back in a minute to take your orders."

After propping their toys up against the corners of the booth, Casey and Petra joined the boys in checking out the menu. It didn't take long for them to pick out what they wanted.

"Now let's see," Amanda began when she returned. "For Matt, it's the usual. What would you like, Darrin?"

Matt started to sputter in protest. "How do you know what I want?"

Amanda shifted her posture, then lowered her writing pad. "Okay. In that case, Matt would like…?"

Matt picked up the menu and tried to look as dignified as possible. He straightened his back, he announced, "I would like The Malt Junction Supreme please."

Amanda smacked him lightly with the menu. "That's your usual, Matt!"

Everyone started to laugh.

Matt tried to resume his regal manner. "But I wish to have a chocolate milkshake with it."

His sister sighed exasperated. "Okay, one Malt Junction Supreme with a chocolate shake. Anyone else?"

When the rest of them had ordered, Amanda retrieved the menus from them and went to the kitchen to get the food started.

"After teasing your sister like that, you had better give her a good tip," Petra scolded.

Darrin started to laugh. "Yeah Matt, don't forget to tip your waiter!"

The comment triggered Casey's memory and caused her to inhale sharply. Everyone turned to look at her.

"Are you okay?" Darrin asked.

Casey was so excited that the words nearly tumbled out of her so fast that nobody would have been able to understand them. Just as quickly, she stopped and took a breath, organizing her thoughts.

"I think I know what the message hidden in the piano meant," she said.

"You know where the treasure is?" Petra blurted out.

"Well, not the treasure, I guess… but I think that I have figured out the clue!"

Darrin tilted his head. "You mean the 'don't forget to…'"

"Yeah!" Casey said, interrupting him.

"Who, what, where…" But before Matt could finish his usual questions, his sister returned with their drinks, cutting him off.

"Matt, they can only answer one question at a time," Amanda said. "Give them a chance to answer the first one at least!"

She placed the drinks in front of them and walked away.

"Sorry, guys," Matt replied sheepishly. "So—"

"I was going to do my laundry this afternoon when Gran showed me this contraption in the wall," Casey started again. "It was hidden behind a panel so you didn't really know it was there. It can be used to transfer items between the different floors. This way you wouldn't have to lug them up and down the stairs. Gran also said that an old hotel like the one we found would likely have a few of them."

"So what is this thing called?" Petra asked in earnest.

As Casey looked at them, the table was so silent that she could have heard a pin drop. "It's called a dumbwaiter."

"Which means?" Matt looked at her in confusion.

"Oh, I get it." Darrin smiled as he looked around the table. "You mean that my great-grandfather was telling us to check out the dumbwaiters."

"Can you tip them?" Petra wondered.

"I don't know," Casey said, "but we can go check it out."

Darrin picked up his sandwich. "Actually, if we hurry up and eat, we might be able to get over there with time to spare before the sun sets."

That comment caused everyone to dig in.

Casey glanced out the window at the sun, which was getting lower in the sky. They were going to have to hurry if they were going to beat the setting sun.

# Chapter Eleven

The sleepy shadows spread across the lawns while the golden sun brushed its delicate strokes of orange, pink, and purple hues over the tranquil horizon. Casey, Petra, and Matt raced towards the quad, still parked in Petra's driveway.

"Can I leave my stuffed toys at your house and pick them up later?" Casey asked Petra.

"Sure thing."

Petra moved toward Casey with her arms already full. Casey piled hers on top and went over to hold the back door open for Petra. Disappearing inside for a moment, Petra soon returned carrying a flashlight and her hooded fleece jacket.

"I could only find one." Petra waved the flashlight. "Do you think we could borrow your grandmother's also, Casey?"

"No problem. I have to stop by there anyway and leave her a note."

Matt climbed onto the quad and started it up. "So who's coming with me?" he yelled over the engine.

Petra jumped forward. Casey had already decided to double up with Darrin on his dirt bike.

Speaking of which, she heard the noise of the bike and glanced down the alley just as Darrin pulled up. Without turning off the bike, Darrin held out the extra helmet. Casey put it on and got on the back.

"We just have to stop at Gran's," she said into his ear.

He nodded, making sure Casey was holding on and that her feet were firmly anchored to the back pegs. He then revved the motor and took off with Matt following them.

Feeling the wind in her face and watching the scenery whiz by, Casey was grateful that she wasn't trying to juggle the stuffed toys in her arms.

Before she knew it, they were at Gran's. Casey jumped off and ran inside the house. Finding the notepad still on the counter, Casey left a brief message telling her where they'd gone—and that they wouldn't be gone too long. She then dodged over to the pantry and retrieved the two flashlights.

Back outside, Casey used Darrin's arm to steady herself as she swung her leg over and pulled herself onto the seat. Then Darrin gave it some gas and headed for the trail that would lead to the ghost town.

They soon broke through the brush and sped down the hillside towards the town's main street, with Matt and Petra in close pursuit. They parked behind the hotel, the same place they'd stopped with the horses the day before.

As Casey got off the bike, she removed the helmet and placed it over the left handlebar.

"Are you ready for this?" Matt asked, grinning at them.

Darrin walked up to the back door. "You better believe it!"

"Do you have any idea where we should look?" Petra asked Casey as they entered the kitchen and turned on their flashlights.

"Well, Gran told me that one of the first places she would look would be either in Mr. Masters' bedroom, or somewhere nearby."

Immediately Matt started for the main staircase.

"It's getting pretty dark in here," Petra whispered as they walked up the stairs, dim light shining through the windows.

Casey had to agree. "I'm really glad we brought the flashlights with us."

Upon reaching the third floor, they walked down the hallway, their footsteps muted by the patterned rug. When they entered the bedroom, they all started to look around at the wood-panelled walls.

"Now let me get this right," Darrin said, looking at Casey. "We're supposed to tap the walls… at about here…" He pointed at a section on the wall that was approximately shoulder height.

"Yup! Well, that's about where the one at Gran's house was located. How about if we each pick a wall and check it? If there's a dumbwaiter here, we'll find it in no time."

They each positioned themselves in front of the room's wall, with Petra helping Matt since they decided they didn't need to check the outside wall. The sound of tapping swiftly filled the room and echoed through the vacant hotel.

"Hey guys, I think I found something!" Darrin called. Everyone rushed to peer over his shoulder. "So now what am I supposed to do?"

Casey stood beside him. "Place your hands on it and try to push in and up."

When he did this, the panelling started to move—slowly.

"Look, Darrin!" Petra tugged excitedly on his jacket sleeve. "Look!"

Darrin started to laugh. "I *am* looking, Petra. Can you point your flashlight over here?"

She nodded and shone the light into his eyes.

"Hey, not in the eyes!"

"Oops! Sorry, Darrin."

Deflecting the light away from his face, Petra handed him the flashlight. Darrin aimed it into the dark cavity, then stuck his head inside the wall to get a closer look.

After scrutinizing the dumbwaiter, he pulled his head back out. They could see the disappointment on his face even before he spoke. "Nope!"

"Did it move at all?" Petra asked.

Darrin shook his head. "It didn't even budge."

Casey wasn't ready to give up yet. "Then we just have to keep looking. Gran said there could be quite a few in a hotel as big as this." She crossed her arms in stubbornness. "I'm not giving up. Think about it, guys—if it was easy to find, why would Edmond go to such lengths to hide the clue to his treasure?"

"You've got a point," Petra agreed. "No one would go to all that trouble with the piano just to leave something out in the open."

"So what do we do?" Matt turned on Casey's extra flashlight as the last bit of sunlight coming through the windows faded away.

Casey looked over at Darrin, wondering if he had a plan.

"We split up!" Darrin said, giving the flashlight back to Petra. "Petra and Matt can check out this floor while Casey and I check out the main floor."

He searched their faces, waiting for an answer.

"Okay, but let's hurry up," Petra said. "It's getting pretty dark out and that makes me nervous."

Matt stood next to Petra. Placing his arm around her shoulders, he tried to tease her into a better mood. "Well, that's lucky… I thought you were going to say that it was because you couldn't stand hanging out with me."

The back of Petra's hand instantly flew backwards, making contact with Matt's shoulder and catching him off-guard.

"Oooph!" Matt raised his hands. "Truce! Truce!"

"Are you guys going to be okay up here by yourselves?" Casey asked. She quickly felt relieved as her friend's anxiety visibly drained away.

"Sure. We'll work our way down to you." Petra glanced over at Matt. "All I have to do is get *this* guy to work…"

"Okay, okay, I get the hint. Off to work I go." Matt started out of the room. "So where do you want me to look next, boss?"

Petra pointed towards the far end of the hallway.

Catching Darrin's attention, Casey led him in the opposite direction—towards the servants' staircase. She shone the flashlight down the steep steps; the beam bounced off the walls as they started to make their way down.

When Casey cleared the last step at the bottom, she turned left and entered the kitchen. She scanned the room, first checking the wall to her right and noticing a china cabinet still filled with the delicate plates and bowls that had once been used in the dining room. Beside it stood a cupboard that held some crystal glasses and porcelain teacups and saucers.

She moved the light in a counter-clockwise direction, until it struck a stack of forgotten cast-iron cookware on a shelf located next to the wood-burning stove. On the floor between the back door and the stove was a crate containing dried timber.

Next, she shined the flashlight towards the pantry entrance.

"Do you think there's a dumbwaiter over there?" she asked.

Darrin shrugged his shoulders. "I don't know, but it wouldn't take us too long to check."

After going through the pantry, inside and out, though, they came up empty-handed.

Casey turned the flashlight towards the last wall and began tapping it on one end while Darrin did the same at the far side. They worked towards each other in the middle.

"Nothing here," she said.

She started down the hallway towards the servants' dining room and hesitated in the doorway, trying to decide if a dumbwaiter might have been constructed behind one of the walls in there.

Suddenly the flashlight started to dim and then went out.

"Oh no," she muttered. "The batteries must be dead."

She played with the switch on the flashlight, then turned on her heel and smacked into Darrin who had been standing right behind her.

"Whoa there, Einstein." His footsteps could be heard as he shuffled across the wooden floorboards. "Wasn't there a window nearby? Maybe there's enough moonlight outside to see… Oww!"

Casey heard Darrin and the groan of the large table as it refused to move from its sentinel spot.

*That's gotta hurt,* she thought.

"Are you okay?"

"Yeah," he said.

From the sound of his steps, though, she was sure that he was limping a little bit. Casey kept listening closely as Darrin patted the wall, trying to find the closed window.

His taps abruptly changed as his hand made contact with the heavy fabric that was hanging in front of the window. Suddenly he pulled the drapery aside and moonlight danced through the room.

Darrin fastened the dusty drape with a tasselled sash that hung on a hook beside the window frame. The moonlight now allowed Casey to scan the room. At first glance, it seemed completely bare of any significant objects.

Then her gaze landed on the long sideboard against the wall on her left.

"A lamp!" she exclaimed.

Quickly, she picked up a kerosene reading lamp that was sitting there and discovered there was still some kerosene left on the glass bottom.

Darrin limped towards her, and she could see that he really had banged his leg pretty bad. "Now all we need is a match."

Turning, she searched the sideboard and noticed an intricate box, made of pewter. One side was covered in tiny ridges, and the top and bottom were loose. She pushed slightly on the bottom and was delighted when it lifted to reveal a couple of matches inside. She withdrew a single match and struck it along the box's rough ridges. A flame burst to life.

Darrin lifted the lamp's glass top and twisted the silver knob to slightly raise the wick. Casey leaned down and held the match to the wick, which quickly ignited. The flame's warm glow lit the room as Darrin placed the top back on the lamp.

She carried the lamp as she moved around the room, studying the walls more closely.

"Can you see anything that might look like a hiding spot?" he asked.

Casey shook her head. "Not in here."

She paused, noticing the wainscoting along the lower half of the wall. There was no other panelling in the room which could conceivably hide a dumbwaiter.

Casey stopped at the window and glanced out at the moonlight streaming through the darkened trees and silhouetted buildings. Feeling a slight chill, she loosened the sash and let the drape fall over the window again.

"Well, there doesn't seem to be one in here." She turned and joined Darrin in the doorway. "Let's check the hallway."

Light from the lamp flickered across the carved timber as Casey stepped out of the room. She stared at the floor-to-ceiling panelling, not sure where to start.

They got to work, each starting at opposite ends and tapping their way towards the middle. Casey checked the wall by the kitchen entrance, gradually passed the servants' bathroom, and eventually came to a stop.

"Hey, did you hear that?"

Darrin rushed over. "Here. Pass me the lamp, Casey. I'll hold it for ya."

As he took possession of it, she placed her hands on the panelling directly in front of her and gently pushed. The panel moved upwards, revealing a dumbwaiter.

Darrin held the lamp close as Casey ducked her head inside and looked around. She shook her head and started to pull it back out when he shifted his grip on the lamp and she noticed something new—out of the corner of her eye, she spotted a small brown envelope taped to the roof inside the dumbwaiter.

"Hold on!" Casey withdrew her head and looked at Darrin. "You got a knife or something sharp?"

Darrin disappeared into the kitchen and returned with a knife in his hand. "Here, try this."

He held the lamp steady again as Casey angled herself, reaching up with the knife to cut the envelope away from the wooden contraption. Darrin then took the knife and returned it to its spot in the kitchen.

She waved the envelope to him in excitement. "Let's get Petra and Matt."

Turning towards the main staircase, she froze at the sound of the front door opening. Quickly she tucked the envelope under her waistband and straightened her shirt. Darrin closed the panelling to make the dumbwaiter invisible again.

Hearing footsteps coming towards them, Darrin blew out the light. Casey felt her panic start to rise as Darrin gently took her hand and started to pull her towards the kitchen.

In an instant, their sight was blinded by a very strong light source.

"So, kids... find the treasure yet?" a voice snarled at them.

Darrin tugged Casey closer to him protectively. "Who are you?"

Chills raced down her spine as a second voice sounded from behind the first intruder. "Don't even bother to lie about it," the voice sneered. "We heard you and your little buddies talking about it at that diner."

The light flashed directly in her eyes again. "Speaking of which, just where are your buddies?"

Casey and Darrin stood still, not saying a word.

The beam lowered slightly as one man spoke to his companion. "Go check out the rest of the hotel and find out if they're here."

The second guy clumped down the hallway towards the main staircase.

"And make sure you check all the floors for them!" the first man bellowed.

Casey prayed that God would keep them all safe and that Petra and Matt would have a chance to hide.

"So tell me," the guy said, poking Casey with his flashlight. "Where's this treasure? And don't even think of giving me a problem or I'll take care of you."

He patted his side as if to show them that he may have a concealed gun.

"We don't know where it is," Casey replied indignantly.

"Oooh, she has a voice!" the man taunted. "And to think they say women know everything… I guess this just proves they don't." He came closer to Casey, blinding her with the light. "You're not lying to me, now are you?"

"No!"

The light changed direction to shine into Darrin's eyes. Casey blinked, seeing dots.

"Is she lying?" the man asked.

"Nope!"

Within a few moments, the other man returned. "Couldn't see anyone else. There's only a quad and a motorbike outside, so they may have come by themselves."

"Fine then. Let's take care of these two and then find this so-called dumbwaiter." The man reached forward to grab the kerosene lamp from out of Darrin's hand and snatched the dead flashlight sticking out of Casey's back pocket. "Now move it!"

Casey and Darrin looked at each other in puzzlement.

The man motioned with the flashlight for them to turn around and head towards the front of the hotel. On their way through the hallway, they passed a bolted door, but Casey didn't say anything.

"Get back here!" the man suddenly called.

Casey stopped in her tracks and looked sideways at Darrin. By the look on his face, she could tell he was trying to keep his emotions bottled up. He seemed to be thinking about the bolted door as well.

"Hurry up!"

As Casey walked back, she felt as if they were moving in slow motion; if the circumstances had been different, she would have entertained the urge to pretend she was walking in slow mo. Now wasn't the time for that.

Or was it? She stopped dead in her tracks and glanced over at Darrin, noting his quizzical expression. This caused her to start laughing.

"Check this out, Darrin." She started to pretend as though she were walking in slow motion. Maybe the fear of being locked in such a small space was making her giddy.

"Cute, but I'm not impressed!" the second man snarled.

With fear, Casey realized that they had opened the door with the bolt on it. Before she could protest, the man grabbed her by her collar and shoved her inside.

The next thing she knew, Darrin stumbled in after her and the door was slammed shut. Her heart dropped as she heard the bolt slide back into place.

She immediately started banging on the door, but it only caused the men to laugh.

"Don't worry," one of them said. "Someone is sure to find you in a few years."

Darrin tried to cheer her up. "Don't worry, Casey. Matt and Petra will come looking for us."

"Yeah, I know."

Suddenly, the sound of splintering wood in the hallway caught their attention.

"Nothing over here," they heard the first man bellow. "Let's check out the other rooms."

Casey groaned as she heard more wood cracking under the brutality of the two men as they continued their search for the dumbwaiter.

"I'm sorry, Darrin. They're ruining your family's hotel."

"That's okay. I mean, hey… at least they haven't found anything yet and Petra and Matt haven't been hurt."

"You're so right. We sure can thank God for that! I just wish we had checked out this door when we did our tour, we'd at least know what we've got in here."

"Well, I don't see any moonlight whatsoever. We're probably out of luck for windows."

She grinned, even though he couldn't see. "But the main thing is that God always has a plan. Now if only He would let me in on it…"

As she stepped backwards, her feet failed to touch the floor and she felt herself falling. Grasping at the air, she tried to grab a hold of something, anything, to help herself stop. She fought the nausea that was rising from the pit of her stomach as blackness invaded her senses.

# Chapter Twelve

Casey groaned in pain as she lifted her head up. She slowly put it back down and instead tried to focus on where she was. Her surroundings were very dark.

*Darrin... Where's Darrin? Is he okay...?*

"Darrin?" she yelled with panic in her voice.

"Hey, you're awake! That's amazing! I prayed that God would look after you and..."

She could hear the concern in his voice. Reaching out to reassure him that she was all right, Casey instead made contact with a dirt floor.

"Do you know where we are?"

"All I really know is that we're at the bottom of some pretty steep stairs... and that you've been knocked out for quite some time!"

Casey moved slowly, her head was throbbing from the impact of the fall. And not just her head; sliding her hands down her right leg, she felt her swollen ankle. She bit back the tears that were starting to form.

"Are you okay?" Darrin asked.

"I... I think I may have sprained my ankle." Wincing, she listened for a moment and found the hotel around them to be quiet. "Did those guys leave?"

"Yeah, they left about..." A little green light shone as Darrin pressed a button on his watch. "It looks like about ten minutes ago, from what I can tell. I sure hope they left the quad and bike alone."

Shifting into a seated position, Casey felt an object in her back pocket. She reached in and found the metal case with the matches inside. She pulled it out and struck a match. The darkness that engulfed them was suddenly forced away by the warm glow.

She was surprised to see the look of shock on Darrin's face. "What is it?" she asked.

"I can't believe it! Do you know what this means?"

She dropped the match as it burnt her fingertips. Watching it extinguish as it fell to the ground, Casey looked back up. "No. What?"

"He answered me twice!" he exclaimed. "He is real, Casey!"

She felt his hands grip her arms and knew that something was definitely going on here, something she couldn't see.

"I'm a little confused here, Darrin. What are you talking about?"

"God answered my prayers!"

Casey was glad she had been sitting down, otherwise the news would have been sure to knock her over. "You prayed?"

She was so excited that it took all her strength not to rush him into telling her all the details.

"Yeah, can you believe it?" he said. "When you didn't come to right away, I got pretty worried. Then I started thinking about how Grandpa always said to trust in Jesus and He will help you. I started to think about how you seem to believe in God and I started to wonder… what if?"

"What if?"

"Yeah, what if everyone had been right all along? Like Grandpa, you, Matt, Petra, your grandma, and Pastor John. What if there really is a God who cares enough to have sent His Son to die for our sins?"

"So what do you think?"

"Well… at first I started to think I was nuts, but as I thought about it… I mean, what did I have to lose by talking to Him? As I started to pray, I remembered Grandpa telling me that none of us is perfect. Only Jesus is perfect and that's how He came to die for us. When I thought about my sins, I felt really bad. So I asked Jesus if He could forgive me, especially for how I've treated everyone since Grandpa died. When I did that, I felt this sense of peace, as if I had been forgiven. So I asked Jesus to come into my heart and make me free."

"Wow! Right on!"

"It just feels so right, you know? But is it really that easy, Casey?"

"Yup, it's that easy!"

"From now on, I want to do things for Him instead of focusing on how I feel." He paused for a moment. "And you know what?"

"No, what?"

"I think God did hear me when Grandpa died. But He took Grandpa to be with Him, and now I realize that Grandpa is happy there. I bet you he's even singing a song to Grandma right now. I want him to be happy and safe. I also think I was angry with God because it was His plan and not mine. But you're right—God *does* love us, and whatever He does is for us. Even when Jesus died and rose again, He did it for us so we can live with Him forever."

"And God cares enough about us that we can know He is always listening when we talk to Him."

He smiled broadly. "That's so true! Cause when you were knocked out, I asked Him to look after you, to make sure you were okay. And then you came to. I also prayed that if He could shed some light on things that it would be great… and you lit a match. Now all we have to do is find something to light."

On that note, Casey lit another match. Spotting a kerosene lantern hanging on a peg above them, she excitedly pointed it out to Darrin. He stood up and retrieved it from its forgotten post, then blew off the dust and passed it to her. Casey pushed down on the slender metallic handle, causing the glass top to rise. She lit the wick and the flame danced, dispersing the darkness around them.

She handed the lantern to Darrin while she tried to get up off the floor. With Darrin's help, Casey hobbled on her good foot to the stairs and sat down. Making sure she was okay there, he turned and shone the light in the other direction.

"I want to go look around. Maybe there's another staircase," he said. "Will you be okay here?"

She nodded and Darrin held the lamp away from them, trying to see into the darkness. All Casey could see was how the light accentuated the cobwebs.

*Oh great, spiders* she thought, her eyes trying to adjust to the darkness as the light from the lantern started to fade.

After just a few moments, though, she saw the warm glow of the light returning.

"Did you find anything?" she asked.

"From the look of things, I'd say we've found the basement storage area." He pointed to the left. "There seems to be a cold room over there. It still has some jars of... I think they were peaches and beets. Other than that, there's no way out of here except through that locked door." Trying to lighten the mood, he added, "But hey, at least we won't go hungry if we're stuck down here for a while!"

She groaned. "You can't be serious! Do you know how old that stuff must be?"

Darrin laughed and held up his hands. "Just kidding. Although I do feel a little bit hungry after all that!"

Casey tried to pull herself up off the stairs and looked towards the top, wondering if she could make it with the sharp pain in her ankle. She sucked in her breath and forced herself not to cry out.

Darrin saw her stumble and rushed over to give her support so she wouldn't have to stand on her right foot. As his arm came around her waist, he smiled at her.

"Don't worry, Casey. We'll get out. Remember… God always has a plan!"

She smiled back and nodded at his encouragement. "Do you think we should try breaking down that door?"

Darrin followed her gaze to the wooden door at the top of the stairs. He motioned with the lantern in front of them. "Why not?"

With his help, they started up one step at a time.

Suddenly the bolt holding the door closed made a scraping noise as it slid out of the lock. The old door creaked open and a light shone down on them, revealing their vulnerability on the staircase.

"Casey! Darrin! Are you guys okay?" Petra was about to start down the stairs, but she stopped when she saw that Casey was hurt.

Without saying another word, Matt hurried down towards them to give them a hand.

Moments later, they were all reunited again. Darrin ran into the servants' dining room and returned with a chair for Casey to sit on.

"It's only for a moment and then we're getting out of here!" Darrin said.

Casey sat down, thankful for the rest. "So those guys are gone?"

"Yup!" Matt looked at the faces around him. "But they sure messed the place up before they left."

Casey and Darrin's eyes roamed over the protruding wood and the splintered remains of the hallway.

"You should see what they did upstairs," Petra added disapprovingly.

A thought suddenly occurred to Casey. "Hey, how did you guys find us?"

Petra gently placed something in Casey's hand. She looked down and saw her necklace in her open palm, complete with the cowbell charm. She raised it and heard it tinkle joyfully.

"The light picked this up in the corner by the door," Petra explained.

"Wow, thanks!" Casey's empty hand automatically came up to her neck, realizing that she hadn't even notice the necklace's disappearance. "I bet I lost it when that guy grabbed my shirt and pushed me onto that landing behind the door. The chain must have broken and fallen off."

"On that note, I think we should get Casey back home before those guys decide to come back," Darrin said.

Casey stood up, shifting her weight onto her good foot, and leaned on Darrin's left shoulder for support. Together, they began to hobble towards the back door.

"How were you able to hide from those guys?" Casey asked.

Petra looked at Matt and giggled. "Well, it's kinda funny. You see, we were at the top of the staircase and about to head down when we heard them come in. I just panicked and froze!"

Matt started to laugh also. "You should have seen our faces!"

"When I realized the one guy was going to come up, I lost it. I'm really glad Matt was there to calm me down."

"So what happened?" Darrin asked.

Grinning from ear to ear, Matt looked like he was going to burst at the seams. "I did the first thing that came to my mind. And I have to admit it... it was fun!"

"Okay, now I'm really curious!" Casey raised an eyebrow.

"He stuffed me into the antique grandfather clock," Petra answered sheepishly. "The one that's sitting at the top of the staircase. It has a solid wood door on it so no one would have seen me hiding in there."

Darrin started to snicker.

"It was like stuffing her into a school locker," Matt said, teasing Petra as he held open the back door for them.

"Well, I'm glad God protected you guys. Who knows what would have happened if that guy had found you two?" Casey turned to look at Matt as Darrin helped her step outside. "So if Petra hid inside the grandfather clock... where were you, Matt?"

Matt became extremely quiet, then mumbled something inaudible as he put on his helmet.

"What was that?" Darrin asked.

But Casey had understood. "He says he was hiding behind one of those three-panelled changing screens. You know, the kind that women used to stand behind when they changed their clothes?"

Petra lowered her helmet over her head, smiling. "Oh! One of those!"

"I never would have pictured you behind one of them, Matt," Darrin teased.

Casey was sure that if Matt hadn't been wearing his helmet right then, they would have seen him blushing profusely.

Darrin suddenly turned to them with a serious expression. "Can Casey double with you, Matt, since her ankle is pretty bad?"

Matt jumped off his quad and moved over to Casey's side. "Sure thing. Sorry, Casey, I forgot about your foot."

Casey tried to smile, although the pain in her ankle was really pushing her to the limit. It seemed that every move she made was touching a raw nerve. All she wanted to do was get to Gran's house and find some ice as fast as possible.

Getting onto the quad without banging her ankle proved to be quite a test, but once she was ready to go, hanging on to Matt, he took off and they were on their way.

Once they'd arrived, Casey saw that the lights were on inside. *Gran's home,* she thought.

As Matt and Darrin helped her off the quad, Petra went inside. A minute later, she came back outside with Gran following.

"Oh, Cassandra dear, are you okay?" Gran shook her head. "Oh... forget what I just said. Of course you're not okay."

Gran stood aside, holding the screen door open while they helped Casey in. They brought her into the living room, then lowered her onto the couch. Darrin even placed an extra cushion under her swollen ankle.

Gran went over to the phone and started to flip through the pages of the phone book. "I'm just going to phone Dr. Peterson and see if he can come over. You don't think you broke your foot, do you?"

Casey shook her head. "No. I think I just sprained my ankle."

"Well, I'll call him and see what he thinks. So how did you hurt it?"

"It happened when she fell down the stairs," replied Darrin.

Gran raised an eyebrow and slightly tilted her head. "When she did what?"

"She fell pretty good, Mrs. Blake." Darrin sat down in the rocker. "She even knocked herself out for a while."

She quickly dialled the number and got to talking with someone on the other end. After the conversation, Gran hung up and came back to sit on the other end of the couch. By this time, Petra and Matt were sitting on the floor near the fireplace.

"Dr. Peterson is on his way over," Gran said. "He wants to make sure Cassandra isn't suffering from a concussion. He said he'll only be a few minutes."

Gran nervously stood back up again and went into the kitchen. When she stepped into the living room next, she had an ice pack and a towel.

"So just how did my granddaughter happen to fall down a flight of stairs and get knocked out?" Gran asked.

"Well, it wasn't her fault, Mrs. Blake," said Darrin.

"Not really," Casey piped in. "I mean, if those guys hadn't put us in there—"

"What guys?"

"I don't know. Two guys who heard us tonight when we were at The Malt Junction and then showed up at the hotel. They pushed Casey and me behind this door and locked it. If we'd still had the lamp and could see, she wouldn't have fallen down the stairs."

"But just think, Darrin," Casey said. "If I hadn't fallen down the stairs and been knocked out... would you have prayed to Jesus at all?"

Everyone in the room looked at Darrin.

"You what?" Petra blurted out.

Darrin smiled timidly and shrugged his shoulders. "Yeah, you heard her right. I guess I'm one of you guys now!"

In the excitement that followed, Gran went over and gave him a hug. "Bless my soul, Darrin Masters, we're proud to have you! Your grandfather would be mighty proud of you also. Actually, I know he is!"

As Matt and Petra welcomed him, Gran returned to the kitchen to make them some hot chocolate.

Suddenly, though, she popped back into the living room with a determined look in her eye. "What do you mean there were two guys who locked you in a room?"

Casey looked over at Darrin, then back to Gran. "Well, they somehow found the ghost town... and maybe they saw our lights inside the hotel and figured we might know where the dumbwaiter was and the lost treasure."

"So they came in and took our lights and locked us behind a door," added Darrin. "Which happened to have stairs that led to the hotel's basement."

Gran looked very concerned. "You know, I'm going to give the police a call. I think we should at least let them know what happened."

She walked back over to the little table, picked up the phone, and made another call.

"Constable Lee will be coming shortly," Gran said when she had finished. "And he said something about trying to locate a missing girl."

The comment started to sink in and Petra jumped up from her spot. "Oh! Mrs. Blake, did you let him know I was here?"

Gran brought over a tray of mugs filled with hot chocolate and marshmallows. She set it down on the coffee table in front of the couch. "Yes, dear, I did."

"Could I use your phone, Mrs. B, and let my parents know that I'm over here?" Matt asked as he stood up.

"Yes, Matthew… and you too, Darrin, if you wish."

"Now why would Matt's parents care if I'm over here?" Darrin asked teasingly. "Er, I mean… yes, ma'am."

Gran smiled back at him, then disappeared from their view again as she returned to the kitchen.

Petra handed Casey a mug and retrieved one for herself. Sitting down at the end of the couch, she quietly talked to Casey as the guys made their phone calls.

Before long, Casey heard the crunching of the gravel outside as a vehicle pulled up alongside Gran's house. A car door slammed and she heard Gran going out to speak with whoever had arrived.

The screen door opened as they entered the kitchen. A two-way radio was on and police jargon was being broadcast through it. They then heard heavy-sounding footsteps as the visitor entered the living room.

# Chapter Thirteen

As he entered the room, Casey didn't even have to see his RCMP uniform; his mere presence seemed to command attention. At 5'9", his frame towered over Gran.

Constable Lee glanced around the room as it had become silent.

"Daddy!" Petra jumped up from the couch and wrapped her arms around his waist.

The constable smiled and hugged her back. After ensuring that his daughter was all right, he reached for his radio.

"You can cancel the APB for the missing children, as all of them have been located at Clara Blake's residence. Over."

"Did you want me to contact their parents, Earl?" a woman replied on the other end.

Matt quickly jumped in. "It's okay, Constable Lee. We just called our moms and dads just before you pulled up."

Holding the radio back up to his mouth, Lee pressed the button. "That's a negative. The guardians have already been notified. Wait, correction. Notify my wife. Over."

"Dr. Peterson will be here momentarily," Constable Lee said. "I passed him on the way."

He had just finished speaking when Casey heard someone pull into the drive. Gran walked out of the living room to meet the doctor at the front door.

"She's in here, Dr. Peterson," Gran said.

Dr. Peterson stepped into the living room and approached Casey. "So this is the patient?"

Casey was still lying on the couch with her foot propped up on a cushion.

"So young lady, what can I do for you?" the doctor asked.

The tall, slim man placed his bag down on the floor next to the couch. He pulled over a stool and sat down on it.

"Let me introduce myself. Dr. Peterson's the name. You can call me Doc, if you wish."

Casey reached out and shook his hand. *He has kind eyes...*

"Cassandra Blake," she said. "But you can call me Casey."

The Doc was about sixty-five with silvery hair mingled with black. Cut quite short, it reminded her of a brushcut. As he reached into his bag, she could see the tan line under his plaid cotton shirt.

*A fisher or a golfer,* she thought. *Maybe a little of both... or maybe a camper?*

Casey blushed as she realized that the doctor could tell that he was at that moment under her scrutiny.

"It's her ankle, Dr. Peterson," Gran spoke up.

"If I may, we'll take a look at that." The doctor got up from the stool to take a closer look. He lifted the bag of ice off the skin. "So how did this happen?"

"There were these guys..."

"...and they pushed Casey and I into this dark room, but it wasn't a room..."

"...and Petra and I were hiding upstairs..."

"Woah!" Constable Lee stepped in as Matt and Darrin both started talking at the same time. It all sounded very confusing, so much so that even Grandma was looking a little dizzy. "Please, only one at a time. Darrin, you go first."

"From the beginning?"

"Yes please. Whatever you can recall." Petra's dad opened up his notebook and started to jot down notes.

"Well, we were out at the old ghost town…"

"Yes, Petra advised me of its location the other day." Constable Lee glanced towards the doctor. "They found the original Crystal Creek on Sunday, just east of here." He pointed out towards the front of the house, towards the mountain.

"Well now, isn't that interesting! I'd only heard stories about a previous Crystal Creek." The doctor shook his head as he inspected the swelling at Casey's ankle. "Never thought it to be true and all. Yes, quite interesting."

Casey began to explain everything that had happened during their last visit to the hotel, including descriptions of the men who had terrorized them. The others jumped in to add details, and all the while the constable took careful notes.

"Ow!" Casey suddenly called out as Dr. Peterson moved her ankle.

"Sorry about that, little one," the doctor said. "I had to check to see if anything was broken. I can still move your toes without much resistance. From the look of things, without an X-ray, I'd have to diagnose this as a sprain. You'll want to keep it elevated for a while, keep using the ice, and wrap it up in a tensor bandage. Just before you go to bed, take off the bandage and reapply it in the morning. And try to stay off your foot for a while. You can take some painkillers, though, and watch for the swelling. If it doesn't start to go down by tomorrow evening, I'll want you to come in for X-rays. All right?"

Casey nodded her head in understanding. These directions were not to be taken lightly.

"Only a sprain. That's good news," Darrin said, running his fingers through his hair. "I was pretty worried after you passed out. *That* was scary."

"You passed out?" The doctor reached into his bag and pulled out an instrument to check Casey's eyes and ears. "How long was she out, Darrin?"

"I'm not too sure, Doc. Things happened so fast. Maybe five minutes?"

"Well, it looks like someone was watching over you, my dear." He finished examining her, got up, and placed his equipment back into the bag. "You seem to have only suffered a slight concussion. Your pupils are fine and there's no sign of blood in the ears or eyes."

The doctor then turned his attention to Gran.

"You'll want to keep a close eye on her tonight. Wake her up every once in a while to make sure she's coherent and knows where she is. If there are any problems, just give me a call. Tight observation!" he stressed.

Selecting a tensor from his bag, Dr. Peterson began gently wrapping it around Casey's ankle.

"Ouch!" she exclaimed.

"Sorry, Casey."

"Sorry, Dr. Peterson, that's not it..." She repositioned herself on the couch and placed her hand over her stomach.

"Did you hurt something else?" Petra asked. "Are your ribs okay?"

"Oh yeah, I'm fine... just fine." She gingerly pulled out the yellowed envelope that had been poking into her ribs. "This is why I said ouch..."

Matt leaned in closer to get a better look at what she held between her fingertips. "What's that?"

"I'm not sure yet." She carefully started to open it, so carefully in fact that she wondered whether she was holding her breath.

"Casey found that in the dumbwaiter just before those guys showed up," Darrin said. "Glad they didn't see her retrieving it."

"You found it in a dumbwaiter?" Matt asked.

"We found one across from the servants' dining room."

Everyone leaned in as Casey retrieved an aged piece of paper from inside the envelope. As she slowly unfolded the paper, they saw a crude sort of map.

"What's that supposed to be?" Petra asked, pointing at a group of triangles drawn in front of two squiggly lines. "What are those lines supposed to mean?"

"They almost look like a picket fence," Darrin remarked.

"Hmmm, it's an odd-looking picture, isn't it?" Gran replied as she gazed down at it. "Is this supposed to be an X over here?"

Huddled together, they all looked closer at what Gran was pointing at.

"There's something written at the top right-hand corner," Constable Lee said.

"What does it say, Casey?" Petra inquired, excitement in her voice.

Casey turned the page around and tried to flatten a crease. Spreading the paper out before her, she could now see that something had been written in pencil. Barely visible, she lifted the page closer.

"It looks like it says, 'Lay not up for yourselves treasures upon earth, where moth and rust doth corrupt, and where thieves break through and steal: but lay up for yourselves treasures in heaven, where neither moth nor rust doth corrupt, and where thieves do not break through nor steal: for where your treasure is, there will your heart be also.' Oh… and it looks like the words 'Psalm 23' were faintly written on the bottom left-hand corner near the triangles."[1]

Casey squinted at the faded wording.

"What? Is that it?" Matt asked. "Nothing else? At all?"

With each question, Casey shook her head.

"That is such a good verse to remember." Gran suddenly got a pensive look on her face. "'For where your treasure is, there will your heart be also…'"

"What is it, Gran?"

"I'm not too sure, Cassandra… hmm, I must have just lost my train of thought. Maybe it will come back to me later."

"There just has to be more than that. I mean, for us to have gone to all that work… and that's it? I don't believe it," Petra stammered. "I just don't believe it. Maybe there's something to the picture on the page. Don't you guys think so?"

"Maybe, Petra," Matt replied. "But it's so vague… where would we start?"

Darrin didn't seem convinced. "Maybe that's all it is. Just a piece of paper telling us that moths and rust wreck things—and if thieves know you've got it, they'll steal it. Great-Grandpa would have had a point to that." He turned to leave, disappointment written all over his face. "Well, I'm pretty beat. It's been a long day. I should get going."

Casey's heart sank for him.

"Yes, we should all get going," Constable Lee said. "I'm sure your parents are going to start to worry a little." He looked down at his watch. "Oh. Before we leave, can anyone describe the two suspects at all?"

They all shook their heads.

"None of us got a good look at them," Darrin said. "Matt and Petra were hiding upstairs and the one guy kept shining the light in our eyes."

Casey nodded in acknowledgement. "Yeah, all I saw were spots."

Constable Lee nodded and started to close his notebook.

"But I think they were both wearing jeans and what looked like hiking boots," Casey added. "That's what I saw when I looked down at their feet, trying not to look into the flashlight."

"Right," Darrin agreed. "And the one had a quilted vest jacket on... dark in colour."

Casey nodded. "And when that guy grabbed my shirt to push us into the stairwell, I banged into him a little... it was a quilted vest jacket... and he had bare arms."

"Tanned bare arms," Darrin added.

"Yeah."

Constable Lee looked from one to the other. "So would you say we're looking for two Caucasian males?"

Casey and Darrin glanced at each other and then both nodded.

"Can you think of anything else?" the constable asked.

"The one guy was taller than me and pretty strong," Darrin said. "I think his buddy was a bit shorter."

"Oh," Casey piped in, amazed at how much was coming back to her now that she thought about it some more. "And the shorter guy was skinnier."

"How so?" asked the constable.

"When he went upstairs to look for Matt and Petra, and when he came back into the room, I didn't hear him as much compared to the other guy. The second one was lighter on his feet."

"That's right, Casey," Darrin said. "Good catch."

Constable Lee jotted down a few final details. "Okay. That's it?"

"I can't think of anything either, Daddy," Petra said.

Matt sighed. "Neither can I, Mr. Lee... er, Constable Lee, sir."

Petra's father looked around at them and smiled. "Good job, kids. And if you do remember something else, jot it down and give me a call. Understood?"

He received a unanimous "Yes, sir," even from Gran and Doc.

Fixing his hat, Constable Lee started to move towards the door. "Matt and Darrin, I can give you boys a ride home... but you'll have to sit in the back." He looked to his daughter. "Petra, you'll be up front with me."

"Do we get to use the lights this time?" Matt asked, grinning.

"I'll think about it. But no siren. Don't even think of asking me, Mr. Barnett."

"Yes, sir" was the subdued reply.

As they slowly filed out of the living room, Casey said goodbye to everyone and thanked Dr. Peterson for the house call.

"No problem, my dear. Just wish that meeting you had been under different circumstances."

She smiled back at him. "I agree."

Gran and Dr. Peterson left the living room, talking to each other quietly.

Casey settled back into the couch and made herself more comfortable. She took another look at the piece of paper in front of her.

*So Lord, what does this all mean? There just has to be more to this page than just a picture and a scripture... I'm sure of it. Edmond Masters wouldn't have gone to all the trouble to hide this. It just doesn't make sense, unless he was into hiding Bible verses around the hotel. Um, I don't think that's it.*

"Did you want a hand getting up to your room?" Gran asked, interrupting her prayer. "Or do you want to sleep on the couch tonight?"

"Oh. Can I sleep in my room tonight? I mean, the couch *is* comfortable but..."

"No need to explain, Cassandra. I understand."

Gran sidestepped the rocking chair and moved some of the other chairs back into their places around the room. Making sure the fire was out in the fireplace and all the doors were locked, she then came over to give Casey a hand.

Casey hobbled up the stairs and soon found herself sinking down onto her bed. Thankfully, Gran had already pulled the blankets back and was at that moment positioning a pillow at the foot of the bed for her ankle.

"I'll just give you a moment to change. Then I'll be back to help you across the hallway so you can get your stuff done in the bathroom for the night."

"Thanks, Gran."

Before she knew it, Casey was tucked into bed for the night. Trying not to move too much, she shifted around to get comfortable with her ankle resting on the pillow. Her ankle still throbbed and she really wished she could have taken a painkiller. But Gran hadn't wanted to give her anything, just in case she was suffering from a deeper concussion than anyone suspected.

She sighed as she pulled her blanket up and closed her eyes.

*If only You could tell us what the page meant, Father. Please be with Darrin tonight. Please help him not to be discouraged but to trust in You. Thank You for watching over us, heavenly Father. Good night, Jesus.*

Hotels, dumbwaiters, playing pianos, horses, bad men, buried treasure, really scary bad men, moths, piano keys moving up and down, rusted treasure, verses... Psalm 23...

Casey tossed and turned, then woke up with a start.

"Are you okay, Cassandra?"

She quickly opened her eyes to see her grandma looking in on her. Glancing around, Casey realized that she was still in her bedroom. By herself. No bad guys.

"I'm okay, Gran. Just had a weird dream."

"Are you sure?"

"Yup." Casey breathed a sigh of relief.

*Lord, please be with me and keep me from being scared. I know that You are my protector. Amen.*

Verses... Psalm 23... the Lord is my shepherd...

And with that, she drifted off to sleep again.

# Chapter Fourteen

Casey woke up with a jolt.

*Psalm 23! The Lord is my shepherd! That verse isn't about thieves stealing…*

She was about to jump out of bed when her ankle reminded her of why she should take her time and move a bit more slowly. She bit her lip in concentration as she eased her foot back up onto the bed. Leaning over, she wrapped her ankle with the tensor Dr. Peterson had given her. The swelling had gone down quite a bit.

She was so excited to tell Gran her new theory that she could hardly move fast enough. Hobbling over to her armoire, she pulled open a drawer and yanked out some navy blue shorts. Next she chose a coral-coloured T-shirt.

Casey turned back towards the bed and noticed a pair of crutches leaning against the chair in front of the vanity. The doctor must have dropped those off in the morning, which meant Gran was already up.

She grinned and pulled the T-shirt over her head.

As she finished getting dressed, she glanced outside to see the sun glinting off the lake. It looked so beautiful out. She just knew this was going to be a great day!

*This is the day that the Lord has made…*

Gathering the sides of her hair, she pulled them together and put an elastic around it. She braided and used another elastic to complete the effect, then ran a brush through the loose hair and let it fall over her right shoulder.

She reached for the crutches, positioned them under her arms, and made her way to the door.

*Nothing like being in a hurry when you feel like a snail could pass you,* she thought as she rounded the bottom of the staircase, only able to take one step at a time on her way to the kitchen.

"Good morning, Gran." She spied her grandma sitting at the table reading that morning's edition of *The Crystal Creek Gazette.*

Gran jumped up and pulled out a chair from the table. "Good morning, Cassandra. How are you feeling this morning? Here, have a seat."

"I don't feel too bad. The swelling's gone down in my ankle… and I don't have a headache!"

"That's good to hear." Gran crossed the hardwood floor. "So what would you like for breakfast today?"

"I think I'd like a bowl of fruit and two pieces of toast please."

"No problem."

Gran placed two pieces of bread into the toaster and took a bowl out from the cupboard. Reaching into the fridge, she retrieved a container that held an assortment of fruit pieces. She set the container in front of Casey, then went back to get the toast.

"You found the crutches, I see."

"Yup. Thanks, Gran." Casey stabbed into the fruit with her fork. "Gran, can I check something out in your Bible?"

"Sure. It's right there on the table." Gran came back to the table with the buttered toast. "Was there something in particular you wanted to look up?"

"Yeah. Last night while I was trying to sleep, I started to think about the verse that was written on that piece of paper. Well, I kept remembering that it said Psalm 23. But sometime during the night I remembered that Psalm 23 starts with 'The Lord is my shepherd…' I wonder why Edmond Masters would have written that."

"That's it, Cassandra… that's what I was trying to remember last night." Gran opened her Bible and started to read. "'The Lord is my shepherd, I lack nothing. He makes me lie down in green pastures, he leads me beside quiet waters, he refreshes my soul. He guides me along the right paths for his name's sake. Even though I walk through the darkest valley, I will fear no evil, for you are with me; your rod and your staff, they comfort me. You prepare a table before me in the presence of my enemies. You anoint my head with oil; my cup overflows. Surely your goodness and love will follow me all the days of my life, and I will dwell in the house of the Lord forever.'"[2]

Casey listened carefully. "Hmmm. So where did Mr. Masters get that other verse from… the one he wrote down on the piece of paper?"

"I believe that verse is found in the book of Matthew. Here, let me see." Gran flipped through the pages before finally spotting it. "It's right here, Cassandra. 'Do not store up for yourselves treasures on earth, where moths and vermin destroy, and where thieves break in and steal. But store up for yourselves treasures in heaven, where moths and vermin do not destroy, and where thieves do not break in and steal. For where your treasure is, there your heart will be also.'"[3]

Casey pondered that. "Isn't it strange he would use one location, Psalm 23, but use the words from somewhere else?"

"Maybe what you just said has something to do with it. Maybe Psalm 23 gives you some clue to the 'location' of the treasure, but Edmond also wanted the person who found the paper to know that earthly treasures aren't worth anything compared to what God has for us in heaven. We won't be using any of it when we get to heaven, so it's better to have God's rewards than store up a bunch of things on earth that'll just get destroyed or stolen from us."

"You have a point there, Gran."

Casey got up from the table and wandered into the living room. She returned with the aged paper and envelope. She sat back down at the table and spread the paper in front of them, trying to make sense of the puzzling map.

"Some triangles over here, some squiggly lines over there… a darker winding line with more squiggly lines next to it. An X near the top of the page." Casey shrugged her shoulders. "I'm just not sure on what it means."

She thought back to the ghost town and tried to visualize it in her mind's eye. She imagined the hotel behind her, with the demolished part of the town in front of her and to her right. The mountains were tucked in on all sides and the meadow was to her left next to the treeline…

Reaching down, Casey picked up her grandma's Bible and turned the page back to Psalm 23. She read for a moment and then looked back at the old piece of paper. Excitement started to build.

She threw her arms around Gran's neck. "You're right, Gran. Look!" She placed the Bible next to the paper. "'The Lord is my shepherd, I shall lack nothing. He makes me lie down in green pastures, he leads me beside quiet waters…' Don't you see it, Gran?"

Gran shook her head. "I'm not too sure. What is it I'm supposed to see?"

"The green pastures!" Casey pointed at the paper. "Oh, that's right. I forgot that you haven't seen the old ghost town yet. There's a meadow on one side of the town, next to the forest's edge. I'm sure that's what those triangles are supposed to represent on the map. They're trees."

"I see. And maybe those squiggly lines represent quiet waters. Possibly a stream or a creek?"

"You've got it! May I be excused, Gran?"

Gran smiled at her granddaughter. "Of course, dear. I'm thinking you'll be needing to use the phone right about now."

Casey finished the last bite of her toast and pushed herself away from the table. Gathering up the crutches, she made her way into the hallway and picked up the phone.

She called Matt first. After quickly explaining her theory about the map, they made a plan to meet. Matt would come over with the quad after filling in Petra.

Now all she needed to do was call Darrin. She said a prayer and dialled his number.

"Hello?"

"Hi, it's Casey," she said a little apprehensively.

"What's up?"

She just couldn't keep it contained any longer. "I think I've figured out how to read the map. I'm not totally sure, but I'm sure that it would be sure if only we could check it out for sure and then we'd know for sure... Surely you understand, right?"

Darrin was beyond speechless; he was confused. "Um, I'm not too 'sure'... I'm a little lost, Casey. Could you please run that by me in English? And a little bit slower?"

"Sorry, Darrin. I just got mildly excited."

"That's one way of putting it, Einstein."

"Okay, from the top. I was wondering last night about the verses written down on that paper. It mentions Psalm 23, but the verse he wrote out actually comes from the book of Matthew. Psalm 23 is the one that starts 'The Lord is my shepherd...' Do you remember it? Or better yet, do you have your Bible there?"

"Uh yeah, just a sec. I'll grab my Bible and be right back."

She heard him put the phone down, his footsteps retreating. A few moments later, he was back.

"Okay, here it is," Darrin responded as he flipped the pages.

Casey went on to explain about the similarities between the descriptions of Psalm 23 and the meadow on the edge of the ghost town.

"The 'green pastures' and the 'quiet waters…'" Darrin sounded thoughtful. "Oh man. What if you're right, Casey? What if there really is a treasure?"

"Do you think you could meet up with the rest of us and go back out there to check it out?"

"For sure!" He paused for a moment. "Oh, just a sec. There's a knock at the front door."

"It's okay, Darrin. It's probably Petra. Matt was going to call her. She'll need a ride over here. And if we use the quads instead of the dirt bikes, we'll have more room in case we find anything that we need to bring back with us."

"Good idea," Darrin said. "We're on our way. Meet you and Matt in front of the hotel?"

"Sounds like a plan."

She smiled as she hung up. Darrin seemed to have really perked up since the previous evening.

The next thing she knew, she heard a knock at the door.

"Cassandra, Matthew is here for you."

"I'll be right there, Gran." She made her way back into the kitchen to find her friend standing at the door. "Hey Matt. Are you ready for another adventurous day?"

"So much so that I've borrowed Dylan's cell phone, just in case we run into trouble again. We should be able to call for help if we need it."

Gran nodded. "That's a very good idea, Matthew. I have to say that it makes me feel a bit better knowing you'll have a phone with you."

"Yeah, Matt, good thinking!" Casey made it to the front door and slipped her sneaker onto her good foot; she let the other be with just the tensor bandage. "I'm ready. Bye, Gran!"

"See you later, Mrs. B."

Matt gave Casey a hand to get positioned on the quad. He also strapped down her crutches, then handed her a helmet. After putting on his own, he climbed behind the handlebars and settled in. He started the motor, and soon they were heading down the trail.

Casey tried to keep her ankle out of harm's way as they made a path through the brush towards the ghost town. The sun was extending its warmth across the little valley and Casey had to shield her eyes in order to scan the area below them. All looked quiet and undisturbed this morning; the town lay motionless in the distance.

Tapping Matt on the arm, she pointed over to the hotel. Matt nodded and directed the quad in that direction. They pulled up to the front of the building to wait for Darrin and Petra to arrive.

"They should be here pretty quick, don't you think?" he asked rhetorically.

"They should be. Petra had just shown up at Darrin's when you came to pick me up."

"So where do you think we should start looking?"

"I think we should start by the meadow." Casey pointed off to the left just as they heard the sound of another quad coming down the trail behind them.

She turned and waved as Darrin and Petra pulled up.

Darrin leaned over and tried to speak over the noise of the quads and around the mouthguard on his helmet. "So where do you want to start?"

Matt pointed to the smoothest part of the meadow. If they drove that way, it would take them right to the forest's edge. "We can decide after that."

Both agreed and shifted their quads into gear.

They drove down the main road and soon turned off onto the field after passing the last broken-down structure on the street.

Casey held onto Matt's waist a little tighter as they progressed across the meadow. She scanned the trees, trying to identify any breaks in the treeline that might lead them into the forest. No luck.

Matt pulled alongside Darrin and Petra and then shifted into park. He took his hands off the quad and lifted his goggles to get a better look.

"Which way do you think?" he asked Casey.

From where they were sitting, there still wasn't a noticeable opening. Glancing back at the hotel, she spotted the window that looked out from the Masters' bedroom and drew an invisible line between that window and the treeline. Based on that trajectory, she mentally calculated that so far their search was off the mark.

Casey pointed off to the right. "Let's try up this way."

"Sure," Darrin replied, turning the quad east.

They all seemed to spot it at the exact same time—a little opening in the trees. Darrin manoeuvred the quad between two ancient evergreens and Casey ducked out of the way of some branches as Matt followed him into the forest that lay before them.

Casey's excitement rose as Petra pointed out the small trail that would lead them further up the side of the mountain. As they slowly made their way up the narrow path, trees loomed all around them.

*They're so tall, Lord,* she prayed. *They must have been growing for years.*

She could still see the sky every once in a while as it peeked down on them through the treetops. But the farther they went, the harder it became to distinguish the trail from the brush—and after a while, Darrin was forced to park and take his helmet off. Matt pulled up behind him and followed suit.

"What do you guys think?" Matt asked as he helped Casey to get off the quad. "It kind of looks like we might have to go on foot from here."

Darrin got off the vehicle. "It sure looks that way—"

"Hey, do you guys hear that?" Petra asked.

They stood in silence, all of them trying to decipher what it was Petra was talking about.

"I hear water," Casey said after a few moments. "And it sounds like it's close by."

"Yeah, I hear it too." Darrin unstrapped the crutches from the quad. "Come on, Casey, I'll give you a hand."

Matt was already walking towards the sound. "Come on, you slowpokes!" he called over his shoulder.

Petra raced ahead to join Matt at the crest of a pine-needled slope.

When he got to the top, Matt looked back at Darrin and Casey and let out a low whistle. "You've really got to see this!"

Casey struggled with the crutches, trying to go faster as she made her way up the small incline and realizing how much she missed being able to use both of her feet.

As she reached the top, with Darrin soon standing beside her, she gazed in awe at the sight before her. There, on the other side of the hill, a creek carried on down the mountainside.

Even more interesting was the path that wound uphill next to the creek.

"Well, what are we waiting for?" she asked as she walked towards the creek. The crystal-clear water bubbled past her as it continued its journey, carrying leaves and twigs as it went by.

Casey looked up at the trail, narrow but still wide enough for them to walk two-by-two.

Matt and Petra led the way, with Matt giving them a tour on the different types of trees as they passed.

"Those ones are pine," he was saying. "And that one is spruce... Oh! And over there, those are Douglas firs... and there's some willow..."

"Do you still have the map on you, Casey?" Darrin asked quietly. "I just want to make sure we're headed the right way."

"Yeah, I have it right here." Casey pulled the map out of her pocket and handed it to him.

Unfolding the page, Darrin held it out so Casey could also take a look. "Well, it does seem we're heading the right way. I guess we just need to keep going this way for a while. What's your diagnosis, Einstein?"

"I agree. Just wish we knew how far."

Continuing on the path, following Matt and Petra, Casey got lost in thought. *How far are we supposed to go, Lord? I wonder if Edmond and Amelia walked along this same trail together so many years ago...*

Petra's voice suddenly broke through. "Are we supposed to keep going here?"

Casey looked up at the view ahead. The mountain seemed to be closing in on them as the path became narrower and rockier.

"What do you think Darrin?" Matt asked.

"Well..." Darrin pulled out the map. "All it shows is an X at the end. Casey?"

Casey peered around Darrin's shoulder to take a look.

"What about that verse again?" Petra piped up.

"Oh yeah." Casey paused, remembering how Psalm 23 went. "'The Lord is my shepherd, I lack nothing. He makes me lie down in green pastures, he leads me beside quiet waters, he refreshes my soul. He guides me along the right paths for his name's sake. Even though I walk through the darkest valley, I will fear no evil...'"[4]

Her voice trailed off as they all looked around, trying to orient themselves.

"Well, we passed the meadow earlier and now we're walking beside the creek," Matt said. "I'd say we most probably have to keep going."

Everyone agreed and soon they had started moving again, although more slowly this time.

Petra walked next to Casey during the next leg of the journey and leaned in close. "I just hope we don't have to go through the valley of the shadow of death," she whispered.

"Just don't forget the rest of the verse, Petra. 'I will fear no evil, for you are with me; your rod and your staff, they comfort me.'"

"Oh yeah, that's right. Thank you." Petra smiled. "I do feel much better now. God is watching over us, isn't He?"

"Yup."

"Hey, come on, you slowpokes," Matt yelled out.

Petra giggled and tried to walk a little faster without leaving Casey behind. "I think Matt's been working with Dylan too much lately. He's starting to sound like him… *slowpokes…*"

"You'll be okay as long as he doesn't call you Amanda or Jenny."

Casey just kept moving forward, trying to keep pace while she pushed ahead on her crutches.

"Awww man!" Matt suddenly exclaimed.

"What is it, Matt?" Petra called out.

Darrin let out a sigh of frustration. "It's a dead end, that's what it is."

Casey hobbled up between them and saw what the boys were looking at—the path had come to a stop at the edge of a plunge pool. A waterfall came cascading down from the heights above.

"No, that's potential," Casey remarked.

Petra excitedly squeezed past them to get a better look. "Is this the best picnic spot ever or what?"

"Oh no," Matt murmured. "She mentioned food!"

Everyone groaned as they glanced towards him.

Petra wandered close to the water's edge and peered down into the pool before her. Here the water paused on its downward course before continuing towards the valley below.

Casey sat down to rest for a moment on a gigantic fallen log, propping her crutches up against it. Darrin sat next to her.

"What are you thinking?" he asked. "Do you suppose the map was meant to lead us here? Petra's right. It *is* a great picnic spot. I guess that could be considered a great treasure, in a way."

Casey smiled at him but shook her head. "Do you feel like swimming?"

"What? Do you?"

"I don't think my ankle could handle it, although I may stay here and soak my feet in the water a bit."

"I don't understand, Casey. What are you trying to say?"

"Well, I have a hunch."

# Chapter Fifteen

"Did you say that you had a hunch?" Matt asked as he came over to listen. Petra brushed away the loose foliage on the log and sat beside Casey.

Casey sat up straighter. "Have you guys ever heard that sometimes, because of the force of flowing water, it can carve out rock?"

"Hmmm, kind of like how rivers can polish rocks and wear them down to different shapes?" Petra asked.

"Or the flow can divert the path of rivers?" added Darrin.

Casey nodded. "Yeah, like that."

"But I don't understand, Casey." Petra twisted her raven-black hair around one of her fingers with a pensive look on her face. "I mean, the creek doesn't look like it's been moved or anything. It's still flowing down the mountain."

"I think we need to look in a more secluded spot."

"More secluded than this?" Matt looked more confused than ever. "There's nothing else around here... it's a dead end."

"What about behind there?" Casey pointed across the pool to the waterfall on the other side.

"Behind the waterfall?" Matt started to kick off his shoes and remove his socks. He took Dylan's cell phone out of his jeans pocket and placed it in one of his sneakers. Before jumping in, he threw his T-shirt atop the pile and looked towards Darrin. "Are you coming?"

"Right behind you," Darrin replied.

Casey and Petra sat on the log and watched as the two guys swam across the crystal-clear pool of water.

Getting up slowly, Casey hobbled over to a large rock on the water's edge. She took off the tensor and eased her sore foot into the water, submerging it up to the ankle.

"How's your ankle doing today?" Petra asked.

"It's still a little sore… actually, it's throbbing a bit right now. Maybe the soak will help. The water is on the cool side and feels pretty nice."

"Oh. I forgot to tell you something. My daddy told me the police are going to question some of the workers at the fair today to see if they can identify any possible suspects."

"I wish I'd seen those guys better to give your dad a good description. Oh well."

Casey's gaze was on the pool as Matt and Darrin reached the waterfall. Suddenly, the boys disappeared from view as they were swallowed by the sheet of cascading water.

Casey and Petra exchange a worried glance and then returned their attention to the waterfall.

"Do you think—" Petra was interrupted by Darrin reappearing through the falls, drenched but smiling.

"It's here!" Darrin shouted. "You won't believe it!"

With that, Darrin ventured back behind the falls, only to emerge again a few moments later with Matt. They were both helping each other lug something that looked like a small trunk.

As they made their way back, Petra reached down to help them drag the trunk up onto the grass beside the pool.

Finding there to be no lock, Darrin pried the rusted lid open with difficulty. When it finally creaked upward, he let out an astonished gasp. Inside lay a pile of ancient-looking coins and documents.

"Wow," Darrin said at last.

Casey smiled. "That sure sums things up."

"Man, I wonder what's in all the other chests that are in there?" Matt shook his head, causing droplets of water to fall off the ends of his sandy blond hair.

Petra looked at them in surprise. "Other chests?"

"Yeah, there's lots!" Darrin said. "I'm not even sure what's all in that cavern. I think we'll have to get some help and bring back a flashlight at least."

"You wouldn't believe how heavy this trunk is," Matt exclaimed. He stood up and examined one of the coins from the old wooden chest.

"Just how heavy is it?" sneered a voice from behind the group.

All four of them lurched around to find the same two guys from the hotel standing right behind them. Casey felt her skin crawl as she saw the wicked gleam in their eyes. She knew what it meant—trouble was brewing. How were they going to get out of this tight spot?

"Tie them up, Scott," snarled the taller man. "And make sure you secure them well."

The difference this time was that the sun was shining and Casey could finally get a good look at them. She tried to memorize as many details as she could. The tall guy had straggly dark brown hair with a bit of a beard. She wondered how many days it had been since he had last shaved. He was still wearing the same vest jacket, which seemed to be dark brown in colour. She guessed his height to be around 5'9" and he looked sturdy.

The man glared at Casey as she sat watching as Darrin got tied up. She couldn't believe how cruel these guys were. The one named Scott pushed Darrin up against the fallen log by the edge of the plunge pool.

"Which one next, Tom?" Scott asked as he looked towards his accomplice.

"The other boy, you dipstick," Tom snapped. He pulled out a gun and waved it in Matt's direction. "As if the girls are going to try and do something heroic! Man, I really wonder about you sometimes."

Scott walked over and started by tying Matt's hands behind his back. Then he did the same to his feet. All the while, Casey memorized Scott's description too. He was about 5'5" and quite slim. It seemed they had been right last night when they'd told Constable Lee everything they'd been able to remember. Scott also had sun-bleached blond hair with dark brown eyes. And he was strong, she realized, easily able to lift Matt and thunk him down beside Darrin.

"Sorry, little lady, but this has to be done," Scott said as he next went over to Petra and began tying her hands behind her back.

"Sorry?" Tom scoffed. "Sorry! Why are you saying sorry, Scott? Man, you're going to give me indigestion. Why don't we just let them go if you're feeling so sorry for them. Hey, why don't we just give them a hand with their little box of money? Better yet, why don't we just go and turn ourselves in and save the cops the trouble of having to go looking for us!"

"Give me a break, Tom, you know what I meant," Scott retorted as he finished tying up Petra and placing her next to the guys.

"So how did you guys find us?" Casey asked, trying to get an answer to at least one of the questions burning in her mind.

Tom was smug enough to reply. "Such a nice quaint town you have here. All you have to do is sit still long enough with your mouth shut and you'll find what you're looking for."

"Such as?" Darrin asked.

"Like how your Dr. Peterson was having breakfast at The Malt Junction and telling his friends how you guys found the original

Crystal Creek and, lo and behold, a treasure map of some sort. Guess I should have searched you before locking you up in that room."

Tom leered at Casey, and it gave her the chills.

*Please be with us, Lord,* she prayed as Scott came over and started to tie her hands together.

"So all we had to do was wait for you guys to show up again at the ghost town and follow you here," Scott said. "Meanwhile, the cops are quite busy chasing their tails by talking to the carnies. We don't even work for the carnival. We're loggers."

Scott sounded indignant as he slung Casey over his shoulder and plunked her down next to the others. Pain shot through her ankle as her foot hit the ground. She tried to bite back tears as her ankle started to swell again.

"So long, kids, and thanks for the loot!" Scott walked over and picked up the chest. "Man, this is heavy."

"Don't worry," Tom said. "We don't have far to go. The kids left some transportation behind for us. Two quads, I believe, with the keys still left in the starters." Tom turned towards them again. "Thanks for everything. You guys have been great!"

Still pointing the gun at them, Tom moved over to his accomplice and grabbed onto one of the trunk handles.

"Let's go!" Tom shouted.

Casey watched as they disappeared over the crest of the slope with the treasure.

"So what are we going to do now?" asked Petra with a bit of panic in her voice.

"We can pray that God will help us," Darrin suggested. He bowed his head. "Heavenly Father, please be with us. Help us to get out of this and find our way home safely. I know You'll protect us, as You have already. After all, no one was shot and they left us alive. Thank You for being such an awesome God. Amen."

In the distance, they could hear the quads being started up. Soon the sound of the running motors faded away.

"Casey, do you think you could move over a little?" Darrin asked.

"What?" She was a little confused. "Why are you worried about comfort at a time like this?"

Darrin sighed before explaining himself. "If you reach into my front left pocket, you should find my pocketknife there."

"Right on!" exclaimed Matt. "We should be out of here before supper time."

Casey moved sideways until she found his pocket. Struggling, she felt inside and quickly located the pocketknife. She carefully removed it and held on until Darrin could turn around and take it out of her fingertips.

After a few minutes of struggling, his hands were free. Darrin immediately tackled the plastic ties around his ankles.

"Stay still, Casey," he instructed as he cut at the plastic that bound her wrists. "Done."

Never had she felt so free as at that moment when the plastic fell away and she could prop herself back up against the log as Darrin worked on her ankles. "Thank you, Darrin."

"My pleasure." His blue eyes danced as he looked into hers.

"Okay, you two, what about us?" Matt whined.

"Well, I guess we could untie him." Darrin smiled. "But we should help Petra first."

Matt started to blush. "Sorry, guys. I guess I just hate feeling helpless."

"That's okay, Matt," Petra teased. "I forgive you."

Before Matt knew it, he was also free and reached to put his shirt back on. Darrin was just slipping his last sneaker back in place.

"Hey, I forgot," Matt said. "I have Dylan's cell phone with me and could get us some help."

Excitedly Matt started to dial. But he frowned when nothing seemed to happen.

"What is it?" Petra asked.

"It's not working. I guess we aren't getting a signal all the way out here."

"Maybe if we try it down in the meadow," she suggested.

Casey agreed. "You guys should go on ahead. Call your dad and let him know what's up. We'll follow you out."

"But your ankle, Casey. It's swelling even more..." Petra straightened up with her resolve. "I'm not leaving you behind. We should all leave together."

"It's okay, Petra," said Darrin. "I'll walk with Casey. You and Matt take off. And if you hurry, your dad might be able to catch those guys."

"Are you sure?"

"Double sure!" Casey and Darrin answered in unison, which brought smiles to their faces.

With that, Petra and Matt raced down the path as fast as they could. In no time at all they were out of view.

"So, Einstein, what do you think?"

"Well, I guess first of all I'd like to thank God that you had a pocketknife on you and we're all free without a drop of blood on us."

Casey grinned at him and he realized she was teasing him about the blood part.

"Yeah, pretty crazy, huh?" Darrin said.

"Pretty crazy."

"Hey, Einstein, you must realize by now that my great-grand-pa Edmond was pretty smart."

"Oh yeah?"

"Uh-huh. You know he wrote that verse on the paper for a reason."

"Which one?"

"Matthew 6:19–21."

"Oh. Yeah, he sure did."

Darrin suddenly sounded contemplative. "Now I see what he meant about thieves breaking in and stealing."

"And moths and rust doth corrupt," she replied.

"You've got it. God's pretty smart too, huh?"

"He knows it all!" Casey turned to look at Darrin as they carried on down the trail next to the gurgling creek. "So what do you think you'll do with the rest of the treasure?"

He shrugged his shoulders. "Not really sure. I'll most definitely get Dad and Mom's input. Maybe put some of it into a museum or something like that. I guess we might have some time to figure it out, unless those guys realize there's even more treasure and go back. And in that case, I can at least say that I had fun finding it."

"Me too."

As they left the dense forest behind and entered the meadow, Casey and Darrin stopped in their tracks. From here, they could see into the ghost town. Four RCMP quads were parked in front of the hotel with their lights flashing.

Casey and Darrin slowly made their way across the field, and eventually they were able to make out Matt and Petra talking to a pair of police officers.

"They must have caught Scott and Tom," Darrin murmured.

"Looks like it, Einstein!" Casey winked at him and gave him a knock on the shoulder. In the process, she stumbled and just about lost her crutches.

Darrin reached out just in time and caught her. "Nice try. But if I were you, I'd wait until I could walk again properly." He grinned.

"Thanks."

Suddenly, Casey noticed that Gran was standing in front of the hotel too.

"Cassandra, are you all right?" Gran asked as she rushed forward. "We should definitely get you off your feet. Your ankle must be positively swollen." Gran gave her a hug. "I'm so glad you're okay. Thank you, Darrin, for looking after her."

"No problem, Mrs. Blake."

# Epilogue

As Casey sat on the couch in her grandma's living room, she reflected on what a busy day it had been. People had been coming and going for hours to get their statements taken by the police, and at the moment Matt was helping himself in the kitchen. Darrin sat in her grandpa's old leather chair, looking quite regal. Meanwhile, Petra was still dictating notes to one of the officers.

In the other room, Gran was talking to the little old lady Casey had seen at The Malt Junction. It seemed that her name was Mrs. O'Reilly. She wouldn't really say why she had been out at the ghost town, but she seemed to have been more than happy to call the police when she'd seen those two villains sneaking around the hotel and giving chase to a group of sweet kids. Thanks to her, the police had been waiting for Scott and Tom when they'd come out of the forest with the trunk. They'd given up without a chase and been forced to hand the treasure over to the authorities.

Needless to say, Darrin was going to be pretty busy for a while, cleaning up the cavern behind the waterfall. Besides, Petra had been right—the area would be perfect as a picnic spot.

Shifting the bag of ice on her elevated ankle, Casey started to wonder what God had planned for her next.

*Maybe another mystery? It'll have to be quite interesting to beat this one!* Goosebumps suddenly developed on her arms. *Okay, God, what do you have planned for me now?*

# Endnotes

[1] Matthew 6:19–21 (KJV).

[2] Psalm 23:1–6 (NIV).

[3] Matthew 6:19–21 (NIV).

[4] Psalm 23:1–4 (NIV).

# About the Author

Sharilee Roe lives in northeastern Alberta, with all four unique seasons. Spring is a blink, summer is gone in a wink, fall is nice, and winter is five months bug free. Her craft time is usually spent with the Sunday school class for which she volunteers. In her spare time, she loves writing, visiting, and travelling. She always has a camera in her pocket, but she isn't partial to selfies.